The Son of the Sun

The Son of the Sun

MOYRA CALDECOTT

ALLISON & BUSBY
LONDON · NEW YORK

First published in Great Britain in 1986 by
Allison and Busby Limited,
6a Noel Street, London W1V 3RB
and distributed in the USA by
Schocken Books Inc.,
62 Cooper Square, New York, NY 10003

British Library Cataloguing in Publication Data:

Caldecott, Moyra
  The son of the sun.
  I. Title
  823'.914[F]   PR6053.A3765

  ISBN 0-85031-647-2

Set in 11/13 pt Palatino
by A.K.M. Associates (UK) Ltd
Ajmal House, Hayes Road, Southall, London.
Printed and bound in Great Britain by
Billings & Son Ltd., Worcester

Contents

I tell you this three millennia
after these events took place.
Mark them well.
They did not end with my death,
and they will not end with yours.

The Threshold

Today the choice is mine: I live or die. When I enter the House of Many Thresholds, the ancient pyramid, the tomb which is no tomb, my duty as oracle is to travel, clad only in my soul-double, to the regions of the gods and there to intercede for my people, pleading for the rising waters, the inundation of the Nile, which yearly deposits the rich black silt on our farmlands, that we may eat and thrive. This year, the year before and the year before that, the waters have not risen at the appointed time: the fields have baked and cracked in the heat, the seed shrivelled, the people died of famine. No ordinary prayers will serve this day. The oracle himself is to be sent beyond the earth, held by a slender silver thread to life, to speak with the gods directly. When it is done I am to return to my body with their answer and live out my life of waiting, my life of service, my life that is no life.

Today, the choice is mine, and I have decided that I will not return. I will kill myself.

That music I hear? A flute playing notes as lonely as my heart.

Am I afraid? Yes, I am afraid. I am Oracle. I speak with the gods; but I have no name that is my own. How will the spirits call me to the weighing in the Hall of Osiris? What name will my heart bear on the scales as it lies beside Maat's

1

feather of Truth and Justice? Like an enemy or a criminal, a name has been denied me: but worse for me, since it has been denied since birth.

It is known that a man is of nine substances. He has his shadow, his double, his soul, his spirit and his body. He has his heart, his intelligence and his power. He has his name. Into life he comes blinded by splendour: into death he goes knowing what he knows. But wherever he goes his name is with him. In the silence, in the waiting and the listening, the cry of the one without a name is lost. Because I have no name I will live no more when I am dead. I will become nothing and will fall back into the void.

I see a star, brighter than any other star, still hanging from Nut's nipple even as Ra rises. It is Sothis, the star that I was born under, the star that should herald the rising waters. I call it *deliverer*, *fire-quencher*, *bringer of life*, but it does not answer. For three years it has been a dry star, pitiless: no inundation has come at its beck, no Osirian green has touched the barley into life, nor drawn the corn shoots from the earth.

They gave me no name in a world where everything is named, but perhaps I, who am nameless, will be named in my death: "Deliverer", "Fire-quencher", "Bringer of life". I will pull the cloth of waters across the world as I die, and leave it as rich as they left me poor, as hopeful as they left me hopeless.

Reflecting in the pool at my feet the star shimmers briefly among the sleeping lilies and then disappears, swallowed by the sun.

Now, it is only as I remember it.

In the west the full moon plunges. The day in which I have chosen to die is with me.

From the dark house the priests, my gaolers, come, padding softly on the flagstones of the courtyard. I hear their voices chiding me, feel their hands pulling me back into the

2

darkness even as the sky bursts into light. Inside, the lamps are still lit because inside it is always night. I should not have been in the high-walled court. I have missed the first incantations, and there is no time to repeat them now. I will have to go on my dangerous journey without the full invocation. No matter. Our words are but the creatures of Time.

I am stripped of my nightclothes, my head shaved, then squeezed into the hard, painted wooden head-dress that tells the world that though I am lesser than the lowliest man because I have no name of my own, I am mightier than the mightiest because I speak for the gods.

I? Speak for the gods!

Why do I not scream and rage, now, while they are pushing and pulling me into their ceremonial robes? They understand nothing of the spirit realms. Some of those they call gods are no more than servants of the Most High, and others are but named aspects and attributes of the One Beyond all Other. The priests teach — but they have not learned. And I? I fear my gaolers. I fear the physical pain they can inflict when I do not obey. But most of all I fear the demons of darkness that they conjure to torment me.

Once again I keep silent. But this time I know that there will be an end to my suffering, to the lie I live. I will not come back from this journey. I will be out of their reach for ever, beyond their filthy spells and their stinging whips.

They never talk to me except to give me orders. How can one talk to a person without a name? But they talk among themselves, and I hear the king himself is to be there to watch the procession and the sealing. Shall I call out to him? Shall I tell him how they treat me, how they lie? The voices I speak with are false, tricks of Ma-nan, the so-called priest. I will tell the king. I will shout out with my own voice that has never been heard outside this house. I will tell him everything. I will destroy my captors. I will pull down their edifice of power. Beggars will spit on them, dogs urinate.

3

Ma-nan narrows his eyes and looks at me. I have never been sure whether he can read thoughts or whether he is just shrewd at interpreting the signals of the face. He looks at me hard and then mutters something I don't catch to the thin one, the one who is always bowing to him. The creature, Pi-en (even he has a name!), slobbers off and comes back running with some thin sticks of that resin I hate.

"No!" This time I scream and struggle, but Ma-nan holds me down, his arms like a vice, my bones almost cracking under his grip. The resin is already lit and the smoke waves in front of my nose. I try not to breathe, but my lungs rebel and finally, after enduring almost unendurable pain, burst open, and I suck in the foul stuff, Set's cursed breath, the dark god's poisonous effluvium.

Ah, but now the pain is gone and I float, float on soft cushions of air. . . . Sleep is near. . . . Do I drift to my golden bed, or do the men lift me? I am as docile as a doll as they arrange my arms across my breast and slip the symbols of my high office into my hands . . . smooth my brow and close my mouth for me. Then a third eye is drawn upon my forehead with kohl, with powdered malachite and lapis lazuli — the eye that will see what no ordinary eye can see. Then the black plumes are set in place at the four corners and we are ready for the tall Nubians who come so swiftly to Ma-nan's call.

I must have dozed off, because now I am in the open air. My body feels numb, and I cannot move my head to see what is on either side of me. I can see the shoulders of the men carrying me, the tall black plumes fluttering in the air, the high, high arched sky, totally blue, totally blank. I try to remember the star Sothis, but even that memory is fading. . . . I taste bitterness with my tongue, but I can say nothing. Ma-nan has played this cruel trick on me before. Inside my head I scream. But no one can hear.

The carrying-bed tilts as the Nubians walk down a ramp.

Without moving my head I can see the crowds now, thousands and thousands of people crushing forward, ragged, dusty, starving, anxious . . . pressing forward to glimpse the great oracle who will speak with Hapi, the great river god himself, and Osiris who will save them from famine. They see me encased in gold, painted with powerful magic symbols. They do not see the one who lives in that house of darkness, a prisoner of loneliness. If they were to look more closely, they would see the tears leaking out of the corners of my eyes.

Level ground is reached, and I can no longer see the people, the parents clutching the hands of children, the youths sidling up to young girls. The tears stop flowing, but I can still feel their uncomfortable dampness at my temples. The bitterness knots in my heart. I can feel the tightness of it squeezing the life out. Let them do what they like; after today they will have no more power over me. I know from experience that the effect of the resinous fumes will last only a certain time. Ma-nan has become very skilled in judging just how much he needs to use to keep me docile for the required length of time. But he knows that he must not use so much that when the time comes for me to "perform" I will be unable to.

Today is a very special performance. Instead of going to the temple as I usually do, I am to be taken to a pyramid, the House of Many Thresholds, and sealed in. There, there will be no priests to harass me, but only my double and the bird of my soul, my *ka*. In death the *ka* is naturally released from the body, and may travel freely through the many realms of matter and spirit, earth and sky. In life, only initiates of a very high order can separate the various substances of their being while they still remain attached to the body. I have been trained for this.

"What if the gods refuse my plea, refuse to give the waters to the Two Lands?" I had asked Ma-nan. "Must I bring this message to the people?"

I see by Ma-nan's face that, as usual, the words I bring will be rephrased by him, cunningly, ambiguously, and without hesitation.

The Nubians stop moving.

This will be because we are about to board the barge that will take us by river to the House of Many Thresholds. There will be singing. The rowers will sing rhythmically and the water will slap the sides of the boat.

There seems to be a longer delay than usual, and my muscles ache with the unsuccessful effort to lift my head to see what is happening.

Suddenly, a man stands beside me, looking down into my face. Beside him is a pale, thin young man whose crisp pleated kilt and golden menat collar seem too large for him. The older man is broad-shouldered and strong, and on his head the double crown fits snugly. The king himself! And, probably, the prince who will succeed him.

Now I should speak out and tell them what I know and how I am being treated, but though my voice, fumbling at first but growing stronger every moment, sounds clear to me I can tell that he is not hearing a single word. I begin to shout and cry and plead, but he hears nothing, sees nothing except the beautiful young painted body with its mask-like face, lying completely still on the bed of gold.

"Look into my eyes," I scream. "My eyes will tell you!"

He stares into my eyes sombrely, and it seems, for a moment, that he is deeply troubled.

The young prince takes a step forward and leans over me, looking into my eyes. He starts, and turns to his father to say something, but at once Ma-nan steps forward, bowing, and speaks to the king. The king and the prince withdraw and I can no longer see them. The bed that is to be my bier is picked up again, and carried aboard. The river journey has begun. *This time*, I think fiercely, *for the last time!*

I listen to the drumbeats of the time-marker, the rhythmic song of the rowers. I listen to the swish and slap of the water, to the captain calling to the steersman. But mostly I listen to my own breath and my own heartbeat, and wonder if, when I come to it, I will have the courage to give them up.

As long as I can remember I have been in the dark house. It has a name: "the House of the Oracle"; but I never call it that. I have been told nothing about my parentage, nor why I have been chosen for this office. I am treated with remote respect by the few servants who work in the house, all deaf-mutes. My meals are brought to me by them on rich and elegant dishes. There is a tutor who teaches me the holy texts, but he will never answer my questions. There is a girl flute-player, but I have never seen her. I don't even know for sure that she is a girl; I just find myself thinking of her as one. Her music is always so haunting and sad I believe that she is not only beautiful, but blind, and I long to run away with her, far from this place, and teach her to see with my visions. Yes, I have visions of my own. Real visions, nothing to do with Ma-nan and his sorcery.

Ma-nan, who is in charge and has been always, treats me with cold severity, and it is he who inflicts pain if I refuse to do what he demands of me. His underling, the thin one, seems as frightened of me as he is of Ma-nan, and avoids me as much as possible. When I am taken to the temple I see other priests, but they are always encased in rigid ceremonial robes and their faces are as expressionless as masks. Beneath the robes and the paint I wonder who the real men are.

Everything that is said and done in the temple is ritualized. The very way the lector priest reads from the holy texts in his high whining voice hides, rather than reveals, any meaning the texts were once supposed to have. How can they expect me to believe the god is really there when they themselves do not address him as though he were?

After the chanting it is my turn to perform. I am placed

before the god in the high place of the sanctuary and am expected to stare into his eyes with the one eye painted on my forehead. I have to stare and stare, unblinking, until my own eyes sting and water in the smoky atmosphere. I am never told the "why" of anything, only that I have to stare until Ma-nan gives me a signal by moving the taper he holds up to the god. Then I have to speak out the words Ma-nan has taught me to say. If I try not to say them, knowing that they are his words, and not the words of the god I am supposed to be speaking for, he will rouse his familiars; and I will be surrounded by ghastly figures, man-bodied, animal-headed, like the gods, yet not like the gods, demon figures who surround me and torment me.

No one else sees them. Only I.

Then, if I have rebelled, I will be punished when I am taken back to the dark house.

I shudder as I remember the punishments. I hear my heart beat faster. I know I cannot go on like this. I *will* not go on like this! This river that bears me now alive, will bear me tomorrow, dead.

We arrive at the jetty. The bier is lifted again. Again the plumes flutter against the sky, as the Nubians lift me and carry me along the causeway to the pyramid, the place where all the worlds meet, the only place I know of where man can leave his body, travel in the other worlds and return to his body, without experiencing body-death.

I shiver as we pass through the low door and into the long gallery of stone. Warmth and sunlight are gone and I will never see them again. For a moment I weaken and think: *A little longer . . . perhaps I could endure this life a little longer, just so that I can occasionally feel the sun's warmth and see its light. . . .*

The darkness oppresses me.

I smell the sticky black blood of the torches, and see the soot-grimed rock ceiling getting lower and lower as we go deeper and deeper in, further and further from the sunlight.

I'm afraid. I don't want to be sealed in. I don't want to be left alone in that impenetrable dark. I begin to scream; but my lips do not move. No sound comes from my throat. The footsteps of the Nubians are enormously loud on the stone floor. I can hear them panting with the effort of climbing up the narrow ramp. I feel I will suffocate long before I reach the chamber at the centre. Huge and grotesque shadows flicker over the walls and the ceiling.

I am going to die with no one knowing my story. No one knowing what I have suffered, am suffering. No one has ever loved me, known me, cared. My loneliness is huge. Having no name, my story cannot even be scratched on the walls, cannot even be written in blood. In my death I will cease to exist. I will never have existed. . . .

We have reached the chamber, and I am lowered carefully on to the slab of cold black granite.

I hear them leave. I hear the hollow clang of the rock door as it is shut. Every muscle in my body is straining to lift me off the bier, to call out, to plead for them not to leave me. The Nubians will listen. I suspect they don't like Ma-nan any more than I do. But Ma-nan's resin has worked well and my body is still paralysed, though my consciousness is agonizingly active. I smell the different kind of resin smell, the kind that is used for sealing. They are sealing the cracks around the chamber door. No one may break these for three days and three nights.

Ma-nan thinks that when he opens the door again, he will find me as he did last time, on the floor, my fingernails broken and my fingers bleeding from trying to dig away the resin and open the door. But this time he will find me lying on my bier as he left me, my face composed and calm: and he will no longer have me in his power. This time when my *ka* leaves my body it will not return, but travel on until it is transformed and becomes spirit, *ba*, one with the mighty splendours of the Secret God who is beyond all gods.

But to achieve this I must keep calm. I cannot die of starvation in three days, and there are no weapons with me to kill myself. No, I will do what I have been sent to do. I will leave my body and travel to that realm where I have been before in soul-form, the abode of the free spirits who have chosen to help our world. There I will plead for the water for the fields, for life for the people of Egypt. When this is granted, and only then, will I plead for myself. If they will not take me I will defy even them. I *will not* return to my body, no matter what.

But first the preparation and the journey.

I try to conquer my fear. I can feel the paralysing effect of Ma-nan's drug wearing off, and I can move my limbs again. The temptation is to jump up as I did last time, and tear at the door. The darkness is absolute. The cold is the cold of the tomb. My heart is pounding. My thoughts race about in my head like rats in a trap. What if I can't control myself, and at the end of the three days I am gibbering and whimpering at the door of life, whining to be let back in?

I waste precious time, weeping.

Now I have the full use of my limbs back. To give that up, voluntarily. . . . I have had few pleasures in this life, but one of them is to sit by the pool in the tiny walled garden of the dark house and watch the water-lilies open. Can I give this up? Can I?

I take a deep, deep breath and bring myself under control. I must not think of the water-lilies, the one star of dawning, the moon, nor of the faces of the people I sometimes glimpse when I am taken to the temple. I must think of the pain, the loneliness, the darkness, the constant harassment from Ma-nan; the demons waiting to get me if I say or do something against his will. . . .

What if Ma-nan has planted his familiars in this chamber? I look around fearfully. But it is as though I am blind, the darkness is so complete. My skin does not prickle as it does when Ma-nan's demons are near. I feel increasingly calm

and relaxed, as though there are good spirits present . . . or
at least. . . .

I begin to do my breathing as it should be done in
preparation for the separation. I flex all my muscles,
rejoicing that they now obey my commands, and gradually
relinquish the use of them, one by one. Every time my old
fear threatens to rise to my throat and choke me I say the
words I was given in one of my visions, words not even
Ma-nan knows. I think, with brief satisfaction, that Ma-
nan does not know how to leave his body as I do, that in this
he cannot interfere — though he will no doubt insist on
giving me the words to say to the people when I come out.
But in here — now — I am alone, and what I experience is
my secret, and the secret of those I reach towards. If only I
can keep my fear under control.

It gradually becomes easier.

I know my *ka* is slipping from my body when I begin to
see again. The darkness no longer exists for me, and I can
see my body as though it is a stranger's, lying on the dark
stone. I see inscriptions and paintings on the walls in
minute detail, yet I know that the walls of the chamber are
not painted or inscribed. To anyone existing only in the
body the dark stone is smooth and unmarked. To the *ka* it is
filled with signs and symbols needed for the journey. This
is the threshold between the known and the unknown, and
there is a map here of the universe beyond the stars, of the
realms where the gods sail throughout eternity. The words
inscribed are not of worldly matters, but are written in the
old language, almost forgotten, hinting at mysteries too
deep for the human mind to grasp. I feel strange — as
though as I look at them they are keys that are turning lock
after lock in my invisible self, and as each one turns, a little
more of me is released from the world I know.

I hover, enjoying the freedom from the restrictions of
the body.

I look dispassionately at the youth lying so still. He is

11

thin. I can see his ribs and his prominent shoulder bones. The kohl has run down his temples where his tears have soaked it off his eyelids. His lips are set in a sad line as though he rarely smiles.

I speak the words of praise I have been taught by my tutor. First to Hapi, god of the Nile, great Spirit of the Inundation:

"Thou who canst not be sculpted in stone, nor seen in the images that are set in the crowns of the South and the North. Thou who accepteth no works nor offerings and cannot be brought forth from Thy secret abode, for the place wherein Thou dwellest cannot be known. Thou who canst not be found in inscribed shrines, for there is no habitation which is large enough to contain Thee . . . nor imagining that can fashion an image of Thee. . . . Whose blood flows with the green waters of the great primeval ocean from which we all come . . . hear my prayer. . . ."

I visualize the river swelling as it does at times of flood, flowing with its rich green and brown over the fields; the festivals of greeting in all the towns and villages; the fleets of little boats decorated with coloured streamers by day, and torches by night, passing from village to village over areas that a few short hours previously had been dry, cracked earth and withered shoots.

And then I invoke Osiris, the great Spirit of Fertility, who will bring from Hapi's waters, and from the rich black silt they have deposited, the bright green growth that will feed the people of the Two Lands.

"Homage be to Thee, O King of kings, Lord of lords, Ruler of princes, who from the womb of Nut hast ruled the world and the underworld. Thy members are like bright and shining copper, Thy head is blue like lapis lazuli, and the greenness of turquoise is on both sides of thee, O Thou god of millions of years, whose form and whose beauty of face are all-pervading in the underworld. Thou art Nepra and Thou givest all green herbs and all flowers. Thou art the Lord of Food, presenting all lands with thy abundance. Grant Thou unto me a path whereon I may pass in peace."

Slowly I climb the ladder of the sacred words. Slowly I say the spells that have come to me from ancient times. The scene around the youth is no longer there. Without passing out of the chamber I am no longer in it. I am in a boat. I look over the side and the water is crystal-clear, and beneath it I can see the continents and the oceans of the world laid out as though on a map. I see my country is small; is one of many.

I drift to the mast-head and see that there are no horizons. We are sailing towards a huge darkness, and behind us I see that we have come from a darkness equally vast. I pray for spirit-sight that I may not be afraid of the dark.

My prayer must have been granted, because out of the darkness looms a huge and beautiful figure. I can see the stars through her body, and feel her breath on my cheek like the whisper of a great and potent secret. It is Nut, who is the spirit of the sky, created before the earth. . . .

I bow as low as it is possible to bow, and my heart breathes the prayer my lips are now too awed to speak. I ask to see Osiris, he who has power to give life on the other side of death. She reaches out her closed hand to me, and as I stare at it enquiringly, she opens it slowly in front of me. Resting on her palm is a golden falcon. He spreads his wings and flutters on her palm, light sliding from his feathers like drops of water. He is a being of light beyond anything I have ever seen. I understand he is to be my guide and my protector. Silently I follow him as he wings away from her towards the darkness. One by one we reach the guardians of the way, monstrous figures, fierce beyond belief, who reach for us — but when the falcon cries the name of Him we go to seek, fall back and let us pass.

"How can such hideous demons serve the Lord of Life?" I ask.

13

"Look back," the falcon says, and as I look the guardian that had seemed so dangerous and harsh is now as beautiful as fire on the hearth. I remember Set, whose other name is Violence, the slayer of Osiris, the enemy of Horus, standing at the prow of the Boat of Millions of Years and in his role as Protector, destroying the enemies of Ra.

We reach the Great Waters out of which the first hill rises. Osiris, green god, rooted in the earth, his branches reaching to the sun, is before us.

How can I speak to such a one? Who am I to address a spirit so lofty? My throat is dry: my words stick in it like bones. And then I remember the suffering of the people without food and water ... the pot-bellies of children with skeletal bodies ... the withered vegetation ... the cracked red earth. ... I forget myself, and pray for them, for the mysterious waters that will bring the rich black earth to my land.

He hears my words, and lifts his hands to receive them, and then he lets them go again so that they drift upwards like smoke ... higher ... higher ... until they disappear into a light-source impossible to look at, so dazzling, so great, that our own sun if placed before it would appear to be a dark hole; our own gods, like moths around that sun.

I tremble, and find myself back in the chamber with the youth who has no name. I remember that I have forgotten to ask for his death.

I can feel his suffering drawing me to him again. Soon I will be back with him, and he will have to face the life he hates.

I am no longer in the world of spirit, but I pray to Isis who has suffered more than any mortal, who has known loneliness and loss. I will pray to her though now I know the gods we pray to, the gods we worship, are no more than mediators between us and the unknowable, bridges that span for us the mighty chasms between reality and reality.

Suddenly, the youth and I are not alone in the chamber.

14

A figure stands to one side of me. He is very beautiful. Not young. Not old. Where have I seen him before? Was it on a granite wall carved by a sculptor with the seeing eye, or is it that he has the eyes of the falcon who was my guide on the journey to Osiris?

"I am Khurahtaten," he says quietly, proudly. The name is unknown to me. His golden eyes watch me.

I look at him, not knowing what to make of him.

"Many things will become clear to you soon," he says gently. "Let my name stand on your doorstep, sit at your table, walk with you in the evening. . . . All things will become clear. . . ."

"Why do you come to me? What have I to do with you?" I ask.

"I seek help."

"How can I help you?" I say. "It is I who need help."

"Nevertheless it is you who must help me."

"But how? I have a body that is kept prisoner by the priest Ma-nan."

"It is a body that houses the soul of a true adept in the mysteries. With recognition will come freedom."

"But now he is lonely and afraid. He does not know who he is. He has no name."

The being looks thoughtfully down on the young body.

"I will help him with my strength. He will grow strong," he says.

I feel the urge to return to my body, to cling to what I know. It is as though I have glimpsed for a moment what we truly are, and am as frightened as someone who had thought he was a child, and finds suddenly that he is expected to be a responsible adult. There is a moment when I have partly returned to the motionless figure of the boy, and partly not. I feel the searing of his pain, his fear returning; yet I am still separate and he screams at me to keep away.

"I won't let you return!" he cries. "Leave me! Leave me!

15

I want to die! I want to die! I *must* die."

His body shudders and jerks as I unite once more with him.

I have failed . . . failed . . . now there will be no escape.

The blackness is oppressive. How can there be such darkness? I, as nameless oracle, struggle to my feet and rush forward, feeling for the wall. I tug the hated wooden head-dress from my head and start to beat my bare skull against the wall, again and again, with all my might. The pain is terrible but I seem unable to kill myself. I remember nothing of what happened while my *ka* was on its journey . . . I can think of nothing but my fear of returning to life.

Blood fills my eyes where tears filled them before.

I join the darkness, and fall unconscious to the floor.

The Journey

My return to the city of Men-Nefer passes like a dream. I
am only partially aware of the sun's bronzed disk low
against the horizon, the river sounds. . . .

Sometimes I am aware of nothing.

Then images swim into view and through a mist I see the
crowd being held back, while the young prince moves
forward to gaze at me. There is something in his face . . . I
cannot tell what it is . . . but it is as though he is desperately
wanting an answer from me and does not know how to
word the question. I see horror and pity in his face when he
notices the blood that has seeped out from under the
formal head-dress and dried on my temple. I look over his
shoulder half-expecting to see his father, the king . . . but I
meet Ma-nan's eye and close my own with a sigh. What if
the king is there or not? What if the prince pities me? There
is no escape. No way out.

In the night the prince is in my dreams. We are reaching
out towards each other through a jostling crowd of people
who are driving us further and further apart. Behind him I
see his father Amenhotep Nebma'atre', and his mother,
Queen Tiye, calling to him . . . behind them is a young
woman weeping. . . .

When I wake I am aware of nothing but the throbbing of

my aching head. I am told that by the king's command I am to be taken at last from this dark house, this place of sorrow. I know not where I am to go, but Ma-nan is agitated and shouts at the thin one. The servants scuttle about seizing things and hurrying them into boxes. For the first time in all the years I have been here routine is broken.

I lie on my bed swathed in bandages, unable to die. Is the move to be a punishment because I tried to kill myself? Is some worse prison awaiting me? Ma-nan, of course, tells me nothing. Through the thundering of the pain in my head I hear snatches of words not meant for my ears, and gather that it will be a long journey. I ask no questions, knowing that if I did, they would not be answered. Worse, my voice would be ignored as though it had not entered their ears, and I would feel again as I have often felt, as though I have no existence except as a tool for them.

When all the house is empty and the echoes double each footstep, each word, Ma-nan comes to me and stands over me, looking down. I cannot read his expression. Is it triumph or bitterness? Only Ma-nan knows how to combine these two. Snatches of my *ka*'s journey have been coming to me, but my head is too painful to sort them out into real and not-real, memory and imagination. Did I do well for the people and Ma-nan in the House of Many Thresholds? I am not sure. I am sure only that I failed to take my own life, and now I am worse off than before because my head is in agony as well as my feet.

I shut my eyes and Ma-nan's face disappears, but I can still sense him beside me. Why doesn't he speak — or go away? At last I hear him clap his hands, and then feet without sandals pad across the floor. The Nubians. Surely not another performance already? But it can't be, because a cloak is put over me and I am placed on an ordinary stretcher, the kind for carrying sick people. The rich trappings of my office as oracle are nowhere in sight, packed up no doubt with the kitchen utensils and the excretion bucket — where they belong.

I am taken through the early morning streets back to the harbour, only a few citizens out to see me pass. Very different from yesterday, when the crowds were staring, pleading with me to bring them salvation. When a prince tried to speak to me. . . .

We board a boat, a sailing-boat of the kind that plies up and down the river for long distances, not the narrow barge I usually travel in. I find my heart contains a tiny shoot, a bud . . . possibly it is hope for a better life . . . possibly excitement that whatever happens it at least will be a change.

The day goes by and I lie under an awning, protected from the worst heat of the sun; the banks slide past. I doze and wake and doze again. There are other people aboard, but they are kept well away from me. In the long dark moonless night I think that perhaps when I am stronger and the pain has eased off, I can creep to the side of the boat and leap off. They will not notice that I have gone until the morning. I can hear Ma-nan's ugly snore beside me. But not now. Now, I have not the strength. I drift off to sleep again. Strange dreams. Someone seems to be trying to reach me. I turn my back on him. I know he wants me to do something for him, but I am too tired . . . too tired. . . .

"Go away," I say, "go away. Leave me to sleep. Leave me alone." I wake and am in a huge night . . . people all around me sleeping, but I alone.

Days pass and I gradually grow stronger. Ma-nan changes my bandages from time to time, and gives me food and drink. He never talks to me. It is as though I am deaf and dumb like the servants. Perhaps I am dumb, I think. I haven't used my voice for a long time.

A north wind begins to blow, cooling the air. A Horus wind that presages the inundation.

I sit up, feeling considerably better. I had thought I had

19

noticed a change in the motion of the boat.and now I see
what it is: the river is running strongly against us, very
strongly. I take a deep breath, hardly daring to hope, and
look closely at the banks. I was right. The floods have come,
the river is on the .nove to cover the fields with its
beautiful, deep, rich, life-giving black silt. I look at Ma-nan,
half expecting him to show some spark of gratitude for
what I have done. I, done? Even as I think it, I know he will
show me no gratitude. Quite rightly. It is not I who have
brought the water. . . .

O Osiris!
They come, the waters of life which are in the sky.
They come, the waters of life which are in the earth.
The sky is aflame for you, the earth trembles for you.
The god comes into being, the god has power in his body.
The month is born, the fields live.

Each night that comes, I think that I should jump
overboard, and either die in the turbulent water or escape.
But each night that comes, I put it off to the next. Is it
possible that I am beginning to enjoy life and want it to
continue? I am still kept away from the others and treated
with cold contempt by Ma-nan, but now I don't care
because every day my eyes are dazzled by beauty. Ducks,
with a green translucence in their wings, fly over me.
Flowering water-reeds shimmer above the surface where
the banks used to be. Flotillas of little boats bob beside us,
their occupants waving joyfully. At evening I am awed by
the splendour of a procession of shining beings accompanying the mighty golden disk of the Sun as he enters his
unseen realms, his hidden kingdom. I never cease to catch
my breath with surprise at the sudden flare of fiery light
that suffuses the whole sky, long after the disk has
disappeared. Slowly, slowly fading, easing us into darkness.
At dawn my heart beats with love, as first light stains
everything pale green like a new shoot, and I see my star

still there when all the others have faded from the sky. The nights are lighter now, as the moon steadily grows from silver feather to polished wing. The only pain I feel now is fear of losing all this beauty, this day-by-day growing intensity of love for the earth and sky and water — the gift of life I have received. When I sleep, I see the one who had wanted to reach me that first night, and I welcome him. We stand on the deck at night with the stars like enormous lamps above us, and he talks to me, telling me that his name is Khurahtaten, an incarnation of the great Spirit, known to us as Horus, sent once before to guide me and now returned to guide me again. He tells me he has a task for me, something that I started when I last lived on earth but failed to complete. He wants me to work with him. At first I argue that I cannot, and then I say "maybe". And now I know I shall.

At first he came only at night when I was asleep. But now he comes in the day . . . at any time. I might be staring at a hawk circling, and I hear his voice inside my head. I might be admiring the infinite shades of blue and pink in a distant mountain range, and he is beside me. I ask questions, and am answered, but I am worried that our time together will be brief and that at any moment Ma-nan may notice the strange trances I slip into, and find a way to stop them. Khurahtaten asks me if I am prepared to take a step from which there is no turning back. Eagerly I cry: "*Yes!*" And then I know that where Ma-nan used to paint the Seeing Eye on my forehead I now need no paint. I am no king, but on my forehead I feel the golden uraeus, the cobra poised to strike at darkness, like the sun. There is no mild recognition, but fission and terror as meaning leaps to meaning, like lightning in iron mountains. Words split in revelation. The crust of my former understanding shatters, and inside, like a geode, my unimaginable crystal landscape is revealed. The myths of my people take wing, and leave behind the shabby trafficking of priest-magic and empty

21

incantation as the golden eagle leaves behind the sparrow. I know my task is to find the living truth behind the holy words and the holy rituals, to bring understanding to a people who have so misunderstood the ancient revelations that they believe the body has to be preserved in Time for the spirit to live in Eternity, and that magical formulae alone can open what is truly closed.

My instructor, day by day, night by night, goes deeper into the truth for which my soul thirsts. His knowledge comes into my mind and becomes my knowledge. I grow in wisdom and strength moment by moment.

Now I do not care that I am kept isolated in one part of the boat, and that no one is allowed near to talk to me. I welcome it, and dread the breaking of my silence. People sometimes come to where the cord is drawn across the deck to keep me separate, and stare at me.

I squat on the deck for hours, unmoving, staring at the blue water rushing past the boat, or stand, still as stone, my eyes fixed on some distant rock-formation from the moment it appears until the moment it disappears. The clarity of the air makes it possible to see great distances, and figures of stone a morning's walk away seem only arrow-far, every cleft and cranny clear.

I presume Ma-nan has strengthened the effectiveness of the cord with some spell, because no one attempts to push it aside and come to me, though it looks easy enough to do. And I, too, make no attempt to escape my confinement.

One day I am standing urinating over the side, when I see that we are approaching a great city. I hear the others on the boat excitedly shouting and pointing, and gather by the collecting together of possessions, the squabbling over position on the decks, that this is our destination. I have a twinge of disappointment. My journey is over and I am still prisoner. *No*, I think, *never again*. I look across at Ma-nan giving curt instructions to his servants, and find that I no longer fear him. I will stay oracle, for oracle has power. I will bide my time, and take this power when I am ready, and neither Ma-nan nor anyone else will know the moment of its approach or be able to withstand it when it comes.

With apparent docility I wait, peering at the great city, Waset. Men-Nefer was huge and sprawling, but nothing like this. It always gave the impression of clutter, as though it had grown up haphazard and too many people had crowded into it. Here there is shape and order. Hugging the earth are the mud-brick houses of the people. Above them rise huge stone edifices, obelisks with glittering pyramidal points reaching to the sun; mighty temple-gates under the protection of the winged sun disk colourful with the fluttering pennants of the pharaoh and his priests; noble houses, palaces with green and leafy gardens beside the waters of the Nile.... Set back on the east side of the river lie the silent hills of pale stone which hide the entrance to the Underworld, the tombs of the kings. And between the river and the mountains the gigantic seated effigies of the present pharaoh, set to guard his mortuary temple. I cannot help being impressed. If I had not seen the king (shorter than myself, though I am scarce full-grown) from his statues I would have believed him to be a giant among men.

I try to re-establish contact with my friend and counsellor, but he has left me alone to find my own way and form my own impressions in this new place. He warned me that he did not want to be gaoler of my mind as Ma-nan was of my body. But I find something of the old fear creeping into my heart as I see the huge walls of the temples, and the darkness from inside lurking behind them. The sun blazes down on them but does not penetrate.

The Meeting

The Inundation has come and gone twice since the day I pleaded with the spirits in the House of Many Thresholds. Ma-nan has found it necessary to control me with charms and hypnotic spells and more and more frequent use of the smoke. Khurahtaten and I have spoken many secret words together, and I know it is almost time for me to show my strength and find my living partner for the task. My spirit companion has told me that charms and spells and smoke will have no effect on me when my time has come, and I must abide till then in patience, storing knowledge against the time it will be needed. When I ask him who my partner will be, he tells me to be patient. He will find me, and I will find him, when the time is right.

The preparations this year for Amun-Ra's journey from his great sanctuary at Ipet-Esut to Ipet-Resut in the south where his consort, the goddess Mut, has her sanctuary, have been as elaborate as usual. The young Prince Amenhotep, in whom Ra-Horus glories, and who will succeed his father to the double crown, is to be present; his father being, at this time, confined to bed with an illness that has been troubling him more and more lately. I have been instructed as usual in the words I am to speak as oracle, Ma-nan manipulating my mind like a puppet with his dark and piercing gaze, his smoke, his incantations. I wait in the darkness of the chamber behind the sanctuary of Mut, dazed, scarcely thinking, the words Ma-nan has fed me lying dormant, to spring forth when he gives the signal.

Idly, my mind's eye follows the progress of the procession of Amun-Ra. There will be thousands upon thousands of people to see the journey; more than usual because of the illness of the king, and their curiosity to see Prince Amenhotep, who was not born to wear the double crown, but became heir only on the death of his elder brother Thutmose, first-born and beloved of the king. They expect the prince to ask for the oracle's pronouncement on his father's health, and for confirmation of his own right to succeed him.

At the quay the god will be placed on a gilded barge, beautiful with fluttering feathers and ribbons, and towed from Ipet-Esut to the southern sanctuary, the crowds following on the towpath, children running and jumping, adults shouting and cheering, traders selling ribbons and fans, and small effigies and amulets. Everyone is happy at last to see the object of their worship — or at least because this is a holiday and the musicians are playing lively tunes.

Once disembarked, the chief prophets of Amun-Ra, now a tremendous power in the state, walk ahead of the procession. The bearers of the jewelled model of the sacred boat in which Amun-Ra sails towards his beloved are all relatives of the king. One is the prince himself, another his uncle Ay, the brother of Queen Tiye. Even Ramose the mayor is related through a secondary princess. The other priests from Ipet-Esut walk behind, while Ma-nan waits with the priests of Amun's consort, Mut, in the great courtyard of their own temple for the procession to arrive — almost as still as the statues of pharaoh-as-god that guard the entrance.

The darkness is very silent in this chamber. I can almost feel it, touch it, as though it were solid. I am seated on a

25

gilded chair raised on a platform, carved with devices from the earliest days, the magical formulae of my trade. My fingers read them as a blind man would, tracing their shapes, bored with the time of waiting. I wish I could see the crowds, the sunlight glinting on the silver and precious jewels of the bark and the divine effigy. I am looking forward to seeing the prince again. I still sometimes puzzle about that dream I shared with him. I have heard that he is something of a weakling, nothing like his father. The rumour is that his father was bitterly disappointed in the death of his eldest son, and barely tolerates his younger. It is to his mother, Tiye, that Amenhotep must look for encouragement; it is said that there are times when she half-smothers him with her love.

I have seen the king twice, once when I was on my way to the House of Many Thresholds, and a year ago at this same ceremony. He had looked into my eyes as I declaimed the words Ma-nan had put into my mouth, and his expression had been very strange. For the second time I had tried to fight the spell I was under and say the words that I believed needed to be said, rather than the words that had been prescribed. For the second time I had failed.

The configurations on the chair are beginning to give me strength. Khurahtaten has taught me many things about the ancient texts, that the priests these days seem to have forgotten. The saying of names is not enough, the drawing of signs, the carving of figures — you have to know the inner meaning of the names, the signs, the figures. As my sightless fingers work I feel the circle that is the wholeness of all things, the spot inside the space within it that is the dimensionless moment from which all things grew. . . . *Who sees, when they see me, that I am Many? Who sees, when they see me, that I am One?*

I find the shape of a falcon's eye and remember that Horus gave his eye to his father, that blind Osiris might see. It was given with love, and with it the seeing is clear

26

and true. There is a left eye and a right eye. The eye of the moon: the eye of the sun. The one to illumine the secrets of the heart: the other to illumine the secrets of the mind. Slowly, slowly I work around the chair as far as my fingers will reach, my mind gradually clearing of Ma-nan's spells as I do so, my own mind taking over.

I hear the distant cry of the crowd and know that I have not much time left. The sign I touch is Maat's feather, that which is weighed against the heart in the Halls of the Two Truths, after the first death, the death of the body. I remember inscriptions on the walls of tombs thought to mislead and placate the forty-two assessors:

> O thou being, broad of stride, who comest forth from Lunu,
> I have done no evil!
> O thou embracer of flame, who comest forth from Kher-áha,
> I have not robbed!
> O thou nose, who comest forth from Khmun,
> I have not been covetous!

On the walls of my tomb, if I have one, there will be no such inscriptions. I know no words can turn aside the last judgement, no green heart-scarab of stone prevent the real heart speaking for itself. It cannot lie, once it is free of its physical sheath, no matter how loud one cries: "O my heart of my mother! O my heart of my mother! O my heart of my transformations! Do not stand up against me as a witness! Do not create opposition to me in the council! Do not cause the pan to sink in the presence of the keeper of the balance!" The secret motives that have lain hidden in the heart will out!

I hear chanting now, and know that the procession must have passed under the protective winged sun above the entrance gate and have entered the great courtyard. Most of the people would have been left outside the walls of the holy precinct: only a few privileged ones are allowed through to participate in the ceremony at the great

27

outdoor altar. The sounds are muffled and very distant. I think I hear a drumming, but it is my own heartbeat. I have decided that this day will be the day I make my stand, partner or no partner.

After what seems a very long time, the pitch of distant sound rises again, and I know the next stage has begun. The uninitiated people will be left outside, and the small group of initiates, including the prince, will enter the antechamber. Prince Amenhotep's training as a priest was at Lunu in the Mysteries of the Sacred Nine, though no doubt he has been instructed in the rituals of Amun-Ra. Once in the antechamber they will all be sprinkled with holy water, while the incantations for cleansing are made. Then they will come into the first hall. Their progress through this will be slow, for they will stop every few steps by some particular inscription, while Na-aghta, a high priest in the temple at Ipet-Esut, and Ma-nan, now a high priest in the southern sanctuary, intone the required words. They in turn go through the required motions, make the correct signs. Once they reach the sanctuary, the chamber immediately in front of the one I am in, the ritual will take even longer.

What are they thinking, I wonder, these priests mouthing these words, making these ancient gestures. Do they think the gods are children taken in by make-believe, enjoying the same bedtime story over and over again?

My hands begin to sweat.

I try to pace out the ritual in my mind so that I will know exactly when my time is come.

Now they will be placing the effigy in its costly boat beside his consort Mut, on the plinth kept ever ready for it. . . .

Now they will be bowing. . . .

Now they will be praying. . . .

Now the offerings will be brought and laid before the god and goddess. I wonder what rich gift the young prince has brought.

More praying.

Now the two high priests will be preparing to lead the prince, in his role as representative of the pharaoh, through the door to me.

I hear Ma-nan breaking the seal that had been placed over the lock when I was led there early in the morning. I compose myself. I sit as straight and still as a statue, the paint so thick on my face it feels and looks like a mask. I hold so tightly to the sign of the ankh, the symbol of eternal life, with the one hand, and to the sign of the seeing eye of Horus with the other, that my knuckles hurt.

As the light from the tapers shines into them, my eyes are momentarily blinded. I cannot see the figures that enter and take up their positions in the small dark room, but I know the prince will be in front of me, the two high priests on either side, a step or two behind the prince. I know Ma-nan will be looking at me, anxious to see whether the spell he has put on me has stayed — confident it has, but checking nevertheless. I keep my face still, my eyes staring straight ahead, trying to fool him.

Gradually my eyes adjust, and I can dimly make out the figures, the small flames grotesquely accentuating noses and the hollows of the eyes. I can feel the young prince's fear at the same time as I can feel mine. We both suddenly know that this is a significant moment in our lives and are afraid of it.

Ma-nan has instructed me under spell to promise the prince the life of his father, in exchange for unbelievable amounts of bounty. But he has worded the list of gifts for the god so carefully, and made it so complicated, that if the king dies it could be claimed that it was because the prince had omitted something from the bargain, not because as oracle I had failed.

Prince Amenhotep speaks the asking prayer, and I notice that his voice is faltering. His face is so sensitive it is almost luminous, his eyes deep-seeing, his lips full.

I stay silent for the required amount of time, taking my cue for speaking from the signal Ma-nan always gives me, the raising of his hand.

I pause slightly longer than usual after the signal, gathering my strength. It is not easy to push aside Ma-nan's powerful spell and I know the effort to do so could destroy my sanity. My companion and counsellor Khurah-taten has given me advice for the chosen moment and I try to follow it, knowing that if my mind wanders a second from the task in hand I could be destroyed.

I visualize a tremendous source of light beyond and outside everything I have ever known, yet infusing everything I have ever known, just as my soul saw it in the House of Many Thresholds, our own sun dark to it.

I visualize the secret source of the river and in its turbulent spring I plunge and wash myself, the water as clear as the clearest crystal, colder than the coldest stone at dawn. I visualize myself rising from this spring washed clean of everything that has gone before.... And then, and only then, I begin to speak.

At first, what I say is no more than the expected words anyone would use honouring the prince and his forebears, but then I startle them all by breaking tradition and standing up. I begin to speak my own words, telling the prince that his father's time for death has not yet come, but that from now on he will not be as strong as he has been, and the prince must prepare himself for the day when he is pharaoh.

"When this day comes," I say in a voice that seems louder than any I have ever known, "when this day comes you will have a task that is mightier than the expulsion of the Hyksos, mightier than the conquest of Nubia."

Open-mouthed he looks at me. I cannot afford to make a long and subtle speech, for Ma-nan is already recovering from the shock, and is reaching into the small pouch I know he keeps hidden in his kilt.

30

"Turn the people round, beloved of god," I cry, "set them to search their own hearts for the meaning behind the ancient texts, set them to listening for the voice that speaks in the silence. Behind the many names of the gods is the one beyond all names. No man can give it to you. No man can take it away from you."

I feel the icy prickling on my skin that tells me Ma-nan's demons are near. I am determined to look neither to the left nor the right, where they are lurking in the shadows, but stare, as before, only into the eyes of the prince. Above his head it seems to me I see the light in all its splendour. I cry out in awe of it, holding up my arms. Around me I hear the rustling of wings and feel the air stir with their beating. Is it Mut the vulture, or is it Horus? With eyes blazing, Ma-nan leaps forward waving the resin smoke that I dread in front of my nose. The instant it enters my nostrils I stagger, my body twitching convulsively, my tongue cleaving to the roof of my mouth.

Prince Amenhotep moves forward, reaching up to me, in astonishment and alarm; but the two high priests take him, one by each arm and, whispering urgently but soothingly, lead him out of the room. He looks back over his shoulder, but I see that his eyes are rolling strangely. It is more than likely the resin fumes have affected him too.

Ma-nan gives me a look of fearful malevolence, and backs out of the door after them, clanging it shut behind him. I try to get off the chair to open it before the bolt is drawn, but I can't move. I am slumped half-on the chair, half-off, and around me in the dark I hear the howling of his familiars and see their ghastly eyes.

"No," I scream. "No! No!" But they are already clawing at me, and my skin is coming away from my bones like the grey rotting skin of a corpse.

The dark beasts almost make me forget that I am man and have within my flesh that which is not flesh, that which cannot be touched by man or demon.

31

"Take my flesh," I cry, trying to stop whimpering with pain. "I don't need it. All that was ever mine I still have, and all that ever will be, you cannot touch."

Why do I see Thoth here, the Ibis head, and Khnum with his potter's wheel consorting with demons? Anubis with jackal-head; the wolf-head Wepwawet, and many others whose presence should give comfort. These are gods from the regions of the other world who should record with wisdom, guide and guard. Why do they consort with Apep the serpent of storm and darkness, Ammut the Devourer, Set and Sekhmet? Round they go, their howling chilling me to the heart . . . demons all . . . all demons! Who shall I pray to if the gods are demons? Who shall be my help when there is no help?

I know Khurahtaten is trying to reach me; like a trapped golden hawk he flutters against the ceiling of the chamber, bruising his wings, his beak like the flashing of a blade moving for my benefit, pecking at an eye here, ripping an ear there. Snarling, my tormentors turn on him and leave me alone. Feathers fall from his wings as jaws snap and teeth tear. His screeching is beyond any sound the ear can hear. There is no human word can give expression to what I witness.

Shuddering, I pull my grey skin from the floor and wrap it round me like a cloak. It warms me, comforts me. It is familiar.

His claws sweep close and then are gone, the flesh of demons dripping from them.

I am alone in the dark chamber, sobbing.

What is the meaning? I plead for meaning. I as man cannot live without meaning. Without it my limbs have no strength, my heart no power. I fall back into the first chaos and know nothing.

Khurahtaten in his human guise stands before me, strong and whole.

"You have seen the meaning of things corrupted. You

have seen the image and the cipher take the place of those truths they were chosen, in the ancient time, to represent. Priests now play the 'gods' like counters in a game of senet: kings move them like the knuckles of their own hands. You have been tormented by the shadows of shadows, the withered shell of a good that has lost its goodness; of a protector that no longer protects; of a teacher who does not understand what he teaches; of a recorder who records what he has not witnessed. . . ."

"Help me to bring back meaning to the gods," I cry.

"I will help you, if you help yourself. I must not play you like a counter in the game of senet. I must not move you like the knuckles of my hand."

"I will help myself, if you help me."

"This bargain is well struck. See — the light is a seal on it."

I look around and the dark room is light. I have confidence. I can see. But Khurahtaten, my counsellor and friend, my defender and mentor, is no longer there.

I look at the heavy wooden door. I know the huge bolt will be in place on the other side. Ma-nan will want me dead.

I sit back in the oracle's chair. I compose myself; calming my breath; straightening my back; my arms lying on the two arms of the chair. My *ka*, half in my body and half out, folds its luminous wings around me like a healing cloak, its head resting on my head, its eyes looking through the door, through the carved walls of the shrine in the sanctuary to the silver statue of Amun-Ra resting in its jewelled boat. Amun the Unseen, ceasing to be as soon as seen. Amun the creator of multiplicity out of potential: become the destroyer out of greed. My gaze is so intense that the metal seems to melt and run, until there is nothing left in the shrine but a shapeless pool of molten silver and a few deformed gems, their crystal shapes mutilated by the jeweller.

My next task is to release the inspiration that in the beginning brought Amun into existence.

My fleshly brows are frowning, but the soul-bird, who rests his head upon my head, is smiling. The joy of recognition darts from his heart to the heart of the god, and, from horizon to horizon, the images of Amun give forth the song they were meant to sing. In temple after temple, horrified, the priests shut their ears, slam shut the doors, trembling as the pillars of the holy halls shake and rumble, the statues of mighty kings tumble down.

Here at Waset in the southern sanctuary I hear footsteps running, and see the priests gathering in the hall, approaching the shrine with cries of astonishment as light blazes out of it.

The shaking of the building dislodges the bar across the door of my prison. Ma-nan and the other priests gasp as I stand before them, the wings of my soul spread above me with feathers of light. My eyes, my own two, and the one Horus has lent me on my forehead, seeing into the roots of their souls, the shrine doors opening, and from them the Unseen gliding away like a breath of wind, the shrine left empty.

"HE RETURNS WHERE HE BELONGS, IN THE ONE."

Are these my words? They come from my mouth like thunder. Yet I have not spoken.

I begin to shiver, remembering suddenly that I have no name.

The eyes of my body gaze across the chamber, and see the young prince once again. He has heard what Not-I said. He has heard.

The wings of my soul are folded in my heart once more.

I walk with careful dignity across the room to the far side that leads out from the sanctuary to the great hall. If I do not look back perhaps they will not stop me. I intend to leave the prison of the temple and go out freely into the great world.

"*Stop!*"

I hear the shout, but do not stop moving.

The prince is close now. He looks pale and bewildered: but he is pharaoh's heir, and no one dare touch him.

"I put myself under your protection, my lord," I say quickly to him. He looks from me to the angry faces of the priests approaching. Behind them the shrine is closed, no longer emitting light. Shadows are gathering close again.

Will he?

He looks back at me, frowning, confused.

"Please, my lord," I whisper urgently. "It is in your gift."

He seems to make up his mind suddenly and straightens up, looking into Ma-nan's fierce eyes with something of his father's commanding strength at last.

"He is to come with me," he says. "He is under my protection."

"He is Oracle, my lord, and cannot be taken from the temple," Ma-nan says smoothly.

"I am son of Amun-Ra and to be pharaoh of the Two Lands. I say he is to accompany me."

Ma-nan tries to control him with the magic of his gazing, but I take the prince by the arm and turn him quickly away.

"My lord," I whisper urgently, "there is danger here. We must go."

He turns with me, and we walk out together.

We both know we are breaking every kind of temple rule and that we are taking a great risk, but he, as well as I, seems convinced that now it is the only course to take. We try not to hurry. We try to give the impression that we are walking out in perfect command of ourselves, and with a perfect right to do so, yet I can feel by the tautness in the muscles of his arm under my hand that he is as nervous as I am.

The priests follow a little way behind. They seem

nonplussed. There is no precedent for this. No rules laid down.

We do not look back until we are safely through the final courtyard and almost ready to pass under the great pylon. Then I cannot resist turning my head to look at my old enemy.

He is standing very stiff and straight, his eyes blazing at me, and, as clearly as though he were saying the words aloud, I hear his thoughts: "You are dead, Nameless One. And in your death there will be no journey to the kingdom of Osiris. You will be dead beyond all death, and I will see your soul pinned for ever to your rotting bones. There will be no going out and coming in. No travelling through time and walking in other bodies on this earth. You without a name, will *never* have a name. . . ."

I shudder. The curse is the most fearsome I have ever heard, and I believe he has the power to implement it.

The Friendship

The long night of my half-life is over. I stand as a free man
stands beside my prince. The sun shines on our friendship,
and he has forged a name for me in its fire and pinned it on
my forehead, that anyone with eyes to see might see it.
"Sothis-who-heralds-inundation": "Star-that-brings-new-
life". Now, when the star's name is called, I answer. Now,
when people ask who I am I say my name is Sothis, and they
go away satisfied, thinking that they have been given an
answer. It has always been believed that without a name
the Spirit returns at death to the great void and is as if it
had never been. The worst punishment a criminal can
suffer is that he be declared nameless: the greatest honour
a man can receive is to be endowed with a new name. From
the words a mother cries out at a child's birth his first name
is chosen. Later, in maturity, another may be added,
expressing what he has become or what he has achieved. In
death all his names are called as he starts his journey
through the Duat. I had thought that because I was
nameless, I was no one, but now I see an earth-name is only
a mask like other masks, a branch to grasp in the roaring of
the cataract; no more. The only name I need, or have ever
really needed, is the secret one I had at my creation as spirit
endless aeons ago, and that no man knows, or will ever
know. It has held me in the Light of the Creator and

identified me to Him. It is longer than time itself, and contains within it all that is and was and ever will be. No man has breath enough to say it: but He speaks it in His heart and knows every nuance of it. When He calls it I will know it is mine, and go to Him. "Lord," I will say, "here I am," and I will speak it for the first time myself, and in it will be all my thoughts and deeds, all my fears and hurts and joys. . . .

As the months pass there are fewer and fewer secrets between Prince Amenhotep and myself. We walk beside the lake at his father's palace at Per-hay and open our hearts to each other. I tell him of the hardships of my life as oracle, and he tells me of the hardships of his life as prince. Sometimes I think that there is not much to choose between them. He has always been a dreamer, a thinker, but has never been allowed time to dream or to think. As a young boy, scarcely adolescent, he was sent to the eastern frontier to learn soldiering. Although Thutmose III and Amenhotep II had secured territory far into Djahi, the peace there was always uneasy and there were always places where corrupt officials had exploited the people, where men who did not know how to love could ease the itching of their disease by violence and bloodshed, where Pharaoh's soldiers, and the boy Amenhotep with them, could learn to kill.

He told me that his learning of this easiest and most degrading of all sports had started in the marshlands of the delta, long before he reached the eastern frontier. The tall papyrus sedges were alive with duck and waterfowl of every kind, geese and herons, storks and cranes, waders on spindly legs, divers and plungers, which the soldiers had great enjoyment in killing. He himself soon became an expert fowler, though the only thing he enjoyed about it was the time he had to himself, hiding and waiting, the sun glinting through the brown-gold puffball clusters of flowers shimmering in the breezes above his head, the columns of sturdy green stems enclosing him like the tall columns of a temple. He could imagine Isis living hidden in these marshes. Amenhotep as a young boy had shivered with excitement when he had heard the tale of how she had sought her husband Osiris, tricked and killed and cast into the sea in a sealed coffin by his own brother Set: how she had found him within the trunk of the tree that had grown round the coffin at Byblos, and how she had brought him back to Kemet and hidden him in the papyrus marshes of the delta. His eyes had grown round with amazement when he was told that she had brought him from death by the power of her love and had conceived a son: no ordinary son but an incarnation of the mighty spirit Horus, one of the companions of the Most High. Once again Set had found his brother; torn him apart and scattered his body across the length and breadth of the Two Lands. Once again Isis had hidden in these same marshes, protecting her son, teaching him her wisdom, that one day he would be able to challenge the dark and re-establish the light.

But the young Prince Amenhotep couldn't hide dreaming for ever, and from time to time he had to return to his companions with a kill. He described to me how his marksmanship eventually drew praise even from the young captain he knew to be closest to his father's ear, Horemheb. This pleased him particularly because he had felt Horemheb's disapproval blowing on him like a hot wind ever since they had set off.

Each night in the marshes they had eaten well, and each morning they had wakened to a cacophony of bird calls, a honking and a squawking, a trilling, rilling and a chirping so loud that some of the men had laid about them with sling-shot and curses. For his part, he had listened with delight, astonished that there could be so many sounds emitted by the feathered kingdom. If he had massed his father's musicians from every palace they would have been drowned by this excitable bird chorus.

The lotuses were in flower, and he had secretly composed a song for his cousin Nefertiti, to be sung on his return. He had no means of writing it down, and he dared not let the others know that he composed songs and poetry. Pharaoh's son or no, they already teased him about his short breath, his thin arms, his womanish habit of dreaming rather than boasting of his past exploits like the rest of them. He suspected that his father had passed the word that he was to be treated no differently from the other new recruits. He repeated the words of the poem in his head as he walked, using it to buffer himself against weariness and the weight of the pack he carried. Suspecting that he had a secret way of escaping the taunts of the others when he limped or lagged behind, the group responsible for most of the cruel tricks played on the young recruits in the name of fun engineered trap after trap for him. On one occasion they very nearly brought about his death. He had been "accidentally" eased into the water, and found himself out of his depth, being pulled down by the entangling water weeds. He struggled silently, trying not to show his fear; his chest hurting, his limbs powerless. The men were laughing at him as usual, pretending to offer him a rescue pole, and then deliberately moving it beyond reach just as he was about to grasp it. Suddenly Horemheb appeared beside them and his heart leapt to think that now at last they would haul him out. Perhaps they would be punished for their disrespectful treatment of a royal prince. But to his horror, as his head went under the muddy water once again, he saw Horemheb fold his arms and stand beside them, watching him dispassionately. Anger mingled with his fear now. It was possible they did not realize that he was drowning and that he could not hold out much longer; it was also possible that this was a deliberate attempt to murder him. Rage and the will to live combined to give him unusual strength. He heaved himself out from under once more, and, his face distorted with anger, strove and floundered until, without their help, he broke free of the rope-like weeds and managed to grasp a bunch of reeds that gave him support and leverage. Spitting green slime and sodden feathers from his mouth he finally dragged himself on to the bank. His tormentors had melted away like marsh mist at sunrise. Only Horemheb towered above him, still with his arms folded, looking down.

"Get yourself back into line immediately," he said coldly. "We are about to move off." Then he strode away without a backward glance.

Amenhotep told me how he had lain on the bank sobbing; how he had looked at the sky and wanted to put a curse on his tormentors, and on Horemheb, that would blast them and their descendants until the end of time; how words had formed in his head so fearful that Set himself would have been proud of them. But something had stopped him. Quiet, strong words had unravelled in his mind like a long golden thread: "More powerful than the curse, the love that unfolds the lotus." He had listened to them with surprise. They were from his own song. He squeezed the mud and water out of his soldier's kilt and knew that he could send the vicious circle of his anger and their cruelty spinning through time, and neither he nor they would ever be free of it, or he could break the circle now, and there would be an end of it.

When he rejoined the others he appeared so calm and composed they looked at him with astonishment. He took his place in the line as though nothing had happened. One by one, over the next few days, his tormentors came up to him, each claiming that it had not been their idea to leave him in the water, but that they had just gone along with the others. Amenhotep smiled. Where was this mysterious person whose idea it had been then, if not a single one of them was responsible? Was it possible they were not lying, that someone else had been present, invisible, sly, deadly,

41

feeding thoughts of darkness to them as surely as he had been fed thoughts of light from another source in the lotus song? Yet they were still responsible. Being fed thoughts is one thing; accepting them and acting on them is another.

It seemed that even Captain Horemheb treated him with slightly more respect than before. Had the whole thing been, perhaps, a kind of test devised by his father to "make a man of him"? He had earned points in the moment he ceased calling for the help of others, and decided to help himself.

Beyond the rich farming lands of the delta and the marshlands and lagoons they had had to skirt lay the desert, and to the north of the desert lay the ocean, the Great Green. He had heard of it, of course, but until that moment, reaching the top of a dry and rocky hill, out of breath and running with sweat, he had never seen it. He was stunned. A water-desert as far as eye could see, a fit companion for the sand plains that stretched ahead of them. Day after day they walked beside it, thirsty, beginning to hate its tantalizing wetness. Sand chafed his feet and scratched his eyes. The sun almost blinded him as it shone off the water. He was not sorry when the route took them out of sight of it for a while. How could such vastness be? Sky and desert and ocean . . . sky and desert and ocean. . . . He began to lose identity, believing himself less than an ant climbing the great pyramid. From time to time they came upon huge statues, stelae and monuments extolling the deeds of kings and their armies who had passed this way, in every case encouraged in their violence and their arrogance by the god Amun.

> *I have come that I may cause Thee to tread down the princes of Djahi;*
> *I spread them out beneath Thy feet throughout their countries.*
> *I cause them to behold Thy majesty as the Lord of Radiance,*
> *Thou shinest in their faces as mine image.*

42

Some had been overturned as the fortunes of war changed, and the sand was already burying them, but the Two Lands were in the ascendant at the moment, and the monuments to Thutmose I and III, and to his own father and grandfather were still standing proud, hardly weathered by the blasting of the sand-winds. Amenhotep wondered if it was because people felt so small that they built so hugely; so insignificant that they carved in stone such absurd and grandiose eulogies of themselves.

The young Prince Amenhotep stayed in the eastern province until he had learned everything his father thought necessary for him to learn, and many things his father would not have approved of his learning. Amenhotep would never make a warrior king like his great ancestors, but he learned enough to talk knowledgeably about troop movements, tactics and provisions. He learned to march, to shoot, to ride. He learned to defend himself in close combat, and inflict death on others if need be. In the early days he hardly saw his father, but once Amenhotep Nebma'atre' decided to visit his eastern dependencies, and the prince was expected to attend banquets, standing behind the king's chair, observing the delicate art of diplomacy. He learned to say one thing and mean another, to hear what was not said, to couch a threat in a compliment and a compliment in a threat.

When his father returned home the prince was left under the special tutelage of Horemheb. The man was hard, and determined to make the king proud of his son. At first, each day seemed longer than the last as they drilled and marched, rode and practised, the few breaks filled with the soldiers' boring anecdotes of how much they had drunk the night before, how many women they had laid since they left home. The nights passed in oblivion brought on by desperate weariness. He despaired of ever having a real

43

life. His limbs ached, his blisters festered, his eyes were red and sore. But in the sixth month after his father had left, when they were faced with a sudden raid from over the border, time suddenly speeded up. He found himself to his surprise remarkably agile and fit, as he rode his chariot into action, even killing without thought when Horemheb gave the word.

Having proved himself somewhat to Horemheb, the captain was not so vigilant, and Amenhotep found, as time went by, that he could get away from the others more often, and pursue a study that fascinated him: the religious practices of the countries in which they were stationed.

There were gods to whom the people sacrificed bulls, gods to whom the people sacrificed rams, gods with the tails of fish, gods that lived in trees, gods of the sky, gods of the earth; Astarte riding on her lion, Baal worshipped with fire. Everywhere he looked there were gods of different shapes and sizes and names; but when he looked closer it seemed to him they were not so different from his own gods, each an element of the mystery of life given features and a name, but not whole as a person is whole. It seemed to him that in a sense a god was an inferior being to a man, for each god had only one aspect, or at most two or three, while a man has many. Huge god may be and man may be small, but in a man's heart lay unfathomable things, distance beyond distance, and time at the movement of a thought. He stood before statues in temples as he had stood before statues in the temples of his own country, and he heard the words of the priests and suddenly he knew; knew why the temples were so oppressive, so dark, so alien.

The true temple for the true god is in the heart. His being is dimensionless, invisible light. It takes up no space, extends through no time. . . . Amenhotep remembered how, since he was a very small child in Waset, he had witnessed the carrying of the god Amun from his

44

sanctuary, his holy of holies, down the great processional way to the river and thence to sojourn, for the full cycle of a moon, in the great southern sanctuary. He had seen the joy of the people, the dancing, the singing, the solemn faces of the priests, the beautiful robes, the glittering jewels he and his family wore as they walked behind the god. He knew that when he was older he would be required to train as priest. But even then he saw Amun's eyes, stone staring out of metal. He knew he should not think like this, this was blasphemy, heresy. He knew that the Amun he saw was only a mundane shell into which the divine could step from time to time if it so wished, and the real Amun was unseen, the father of the gods, the Great One, the Mighty. But everywhere he went, each country claimed this for their god or their goddess. He saw many Great Ones worshipped, many Mighty.

He walked by a great river far from his homeland, and his thoughts thrashed about like a trapped animal. At last, wearily, he sat on a rock at the water's edge and watched the image of the sun dancing in the water in front of him, its reflection distorting its true shape, ripples causing it to break up and appear as many different images. He looked up to the magnificent arc of the heavens, tried to look directly at the sun itself. Instantly the pain made him shut his eyes. An after-image of the fire danced on the inside of his lids. He remembered the words that are written in the book for all those who leave this earth and travel in the Duat — the guide who leads the being through all the transformations necessary for life beyond life: "He is not the Sun of this or that moment, but of yesterday, today, and of all eternity, the 'One proceeding from the One'. We call him Ra-Harakti at dawn, Khepra at noon, and Atum as he sinks below the horizon in the west; and in all the naming we forget he is none of these but mysteriously, powerfully, ultimately the One proceeding from the One."

When he tells me of this vision I am tremendously

excited. Now there is no doubt in my heart that he is partner with me in the great task that Khurahtaten has set us.

"*Sothis!*" My prince calls my new earth-name and I go to him. We walk beside the lake in the cool air before dawn, the last stars like flecks of light in lapis lazuli. I remember how Khurahtaten has told me that lapis lazuli was brought from the east where the sun rises and used for the eyes of the gods, not because it has magic properties in itself, but because it reminded our forefathers of the deep blue sky of evening and of the dawn: the times when the invisible sometimes becomes visible.

I see that my prince is troubled. He has taken me from my prison and I love him for it. His trouble is my trouble. He is pacing beside the lake, and I can see that he has not noticed the mother-of-pearl sheen on the water turning to molten gold as the sun suddenly bursts over the eastern desert. He has not noticed the tall obelisks tipped with gold, igniting with the sun's light like a line of running fire. A kingfisher hovers, and then dives so cleanly that scarcely a ripple shows where his beak has entered the water. He rises again with a struggling blue and silver fish.

"What is it, my lord?" I ask quietly, not wanting to break the fragile mood of the dawn, but knowing that he needs to be asked. He looks up at me thoughtfully.

"There are so many things I want to know — so many things I need to know," he says, "but life goes by too fast and now. . . ." He pauses, frowning.

"And now?" I prompt.

"And now it seems I am to be king before I am ready."

I look surprised.

"Is the King's condition worse?" I ask.

Amenhotep shakes his head.

"No, not worse," he says, "but last night he called me to his room and spoke to me in a way —" he hesitates — "in a

46

way I had never thought to hear him speak."

I wait patiently, knowing that I will be told.

"His fever had broken, and he seemed quite calm and relaxed. It was better than the time before," Amenhotep says. He has told me of his father's strange fantasies when his fever was high, when even the touch of his queen, Tiye, whom he loved beyond all others, offended him, and the intoning of prayers and spells by the priests drove him crazy with rage. He had spoken then as though he didn't know whether he were alive or dead, confusing his feverish dreams with his journey through the Duat after death; calling his pleasure lake at Per-hay, the "Great Lake of Peace", and claiming that the barge named *Aten Gleams* was in fact a spirit-barge ferrying him to the kingdom of Osiris. Was it Horus himself, Lord of the Sun and of the Two Lands, or a hawk, circling over him with outspread golden wings? Were the stars he saw the jewels of Nut — the spirit-lamps in the throne-room of Osiris where he would face the Great Judgment — or the flickering candles lit by Tiye in his room at Per-hay? Sometimes, the creature lurking in the corner looked like Ammut, the hideous Devourer of those souls that had failed to satisfy Maat and the forty-two assessors, and at other times like one of his own physicians.

Now he was tired, and longed for rest. The burden of being god-who-walked-on-earth was sometimes too much, and this was one of those times. He was weary of being the fulcrum on which the invisible and the visible turned, the shoulders that bore the teeming millions of the earth. When he was young and strong, dressed in his full regalia with his crown upon his head, everyone bowing, everyone listening to every word he said, and jumping to carry out his commands, it had seemed an easy and a pleasant thing to be a divine king. As he grew older and less arrogant he had realized that he, the man who grew tired and angry and disillusioned, was very far from being a god . . . but the pretence had to be kept up.

Amenhotep pauses. He is obviously deeply moved by his father's confidences, but he has reached a point in the telling of them where he thinks perhaps he should be silent. Again I wait.

"He hinted that he had done things at one time that he was now ashamed of." I tell him that he must not reveal to me what his father had said, if he thinks it wrong.

"There was a moment when I thought he was going to tell me something about you," my friend says, and looks at me for a moment doubtfully. My heart skips a beat, but I say nothing. "He has never approved of my bringing you here," he continues. "I've never understood it. It is almost as though . . . almost as though he fears you in some way." Amenhotep looks at me very closely. "Should he?"

I shake my head. "I can think of no reason why he should."

"Nor can I," he says, suddenly with conviction.

"What did he say?"

"Oh, it wasn't anything . . . his mind seemed to wander for a moment, and then he was quite clear again, and talked about how, after his illness, he feared he would not be vigorous enough again to shoulder the full burden of the two crowns. He said he felt it was time to share the government with me."

"A co-regency?"

"Yes."

I pace beside him in silence. I know he is not ready to be king. But regent? How would this affect the task Khurah-taten had set us both, the task of opening the mouth of dead ritual, that the living truth might be heard again in our land?

We hear a call and turn at the lake edge, both finding it difficult to leave our thoughts. From the flowering terraces in front of the palace we see the figure of a young girl running towards us, fine pleated muslin billowing out like a

48

sail behind her, the curves of her figure as beautiful as Hathor's, the lady of the southern sycamores.

My pulse quickens. Nefertiti, whose name means "the beautiful one comes": Nefertiti, beloved of Amenhotep, daughter of his uncle Ay and his first wife.

We begin to walk to meet her. Her cheeks are flushed with the exertion of running, her eyes alight with the news she carries. She flings her arms about him and dances him around, laughing with delight.

"You'll never believe the good news I bring!" she cries. Her dark eyes are the night sky at full moon, her hair a raven's wing. He holds her and kisses her. I notice her breasts — yes, her breasts.

I ache. And turn away.

"The marriage is arranged at last! After the next full moon we'll never be parted again," she sings.

I don't hear his reply. I step closer to the lake, stoop down and pick up some pebbles, and start to skim them across the water. A heron, standing sombrely on a rock surveying the scene, flies up with a loud and indignant cry, and wings away low over the water.

But they insist on sharing their joy with me. They put their arms around me and make me dance with them along the shore, singing a ridiculous, happy song. Tears are running down both their cheeks. They have been in love as long as they can remember, but there had been talk that Amenhotep would have to take another as his Great Royal Wife because Nefertiti, through her Mycenaean mother, had foreign blood in her veins. Now the king must have relented, perhaps persuaded by Queen Tiye, whose brother was Nefertiti's father, and who indulged her son Amenhotep whenever she could.

The prince is not handsome. He is too thin, his chin too long, his lips too thick; but Nefertiti loves him and in her love he becomes beautiful.

I am handsome. I am tall and well-proportioned, my

49

features regular. But, because Nefertiti does not notice me
— I am ugly.

As soon as he is declared co-regent at his father's Sed
festival, the prince takes the names Nefer-khepru-ré
Wa'en-ré Amenhotep: Amenhotep IV. He begins to plan a
new temple at Ipet-Esut, to the rising sun — Ra Harakti —
which he hopes will rival the might and splendour of the
great temple of Amun close beside it. The dedication in this
temple is the first public hint he gives that there is to be a
change in the way the gods are viewed.

He uses the name Aten frequently, as the one closest to
what he wants to express, pleasing his mother and
father who have always had an affection for this ancient
sun-god, but who do not realise that his concept of it is
slightly different from their own. He is watched closely
by the priests of Amun, jealous of their privileged position
as custodians of the Two Lands' currently most powerful
god.

He also builds his queen a separate palace. They use
mud-brick and painted plaster, and tile the floors with
lively, colourful ceramic tiles. It becomes a cheerful place to
be, the evenings noisy with young people enjoying themselves. Amenhotep himself is not particularly interested in
the revelry, but Nefertiti enjoys every moment of it. He
tends to carry on long, rambling discussions about the new
theories of art and religion he is trying to introduce, with
anyone who will listen, while she is enjoying the dancing
and the music, passing among her guests like a butterfly
with brilliant wings.

It seems to them a new age is about to begin, and they are
set to change the world. I share in all their plans and all
their hopes, but sometimes wonder if their enthusiasm is
not blinding them to difficulties and dangers.

The temple to Ra-Harakti at Ipet-Esut is not to have
darkly roofed halls, though there will be colonnades for

shade. The worship of Aten will be in the open air, and the altar for offerings is to be placed so that at no time during the day will the sun's rays leave it. There is no dark and secret inner sanctuary where the god will be kept behind closed doors.

"His sanctuary is everywhere," Amenhotep declares, waving his arms to indicate the desert cliffs, the green and fruitful strip of land beside the river, and the wide and arching skies above. This brings uneasy mutterings from those who are used to the sun-god in his other forms; vividly portrayed on stone and papyrus, and available in handy amulet form.

But as the shining sandstone columns rise, the pylons receive their fluttering pennants, the obelisks their caps of gold, young Amenhotep seems unaware of the under-current of dissension. He surrounds himself only with his friends, people who find excitement in the new ideas and have hope for the new age. Throughout the land new temples to Aten are built, old ones refurbished.

Nefertiti is pregnant, and gives birth to a daughter. They call her Meryt-aten, and carry her at once to the new temple, though it is scarcely finished, to lift her in their arms above the altar and dedicate her to the deity they believe was before all others, the mysterious one, the great He-She, symbolized by the light of the sun.

After two other daughters have been born, Maket-aten and Ankhesenpa-aten, and have been blessed in the new temple of Aten at Ipet-Esut, I am told that a new city is to be established on virgin ground, halfway between Waset and Men-Nefer: a threshold sacred only to the Aten, free of the clinging spells and the dark ghosts that haunt the environs of Amun's temple.

At Ipet-Esut the two temples are separate, and the worship of Amun and his family, Mut and Khons, goes on unhindered as before; only the young friends of the co-regent and his wife shun their precincts entirely. The old king still worships in the traditional way the traditional gods, and pays as much tribute to Amun as before, but he sometimes honours us with his presence. I am often disturbed by the way he looks at me. What is he thinking? His queen, Tiye, seems to dislike me and does everything in her power to discourage my close friendship with her son. Once, in a dark alley, someone tried to knife me. I had no reason to believe that she was behind the would-be assassin, though the thought did cross my mind. It would have been more reasonable to suspect my old enemies.

I have not seen Ma-nan for years, for the prince had banished him under strong guard to Nubia soon after he had given me my freedom, but I am very much aware that Na-aghta of the Temple of Amun is my enemy. He does not attack me openly, because I am the favourite of the co-regent. His position is not as secure as it used to be, and he takes care to ingratiate himself with the old king, while leaving the co-regent and his protégé well alone. I see by his eyes when I meet him that he has not forgotten the incident in Mut's temple, and is biding his time for revenge. I often ponder what went wrong with the worship of Amun, and at what point human corruption destroyed the ancient archetype.

Sometimes, at night, I feel that malevolent spells are reaching me. My childhood fears return and I sense Ma-nan's familiars around me. But now I have Aten's strength, and prayers that are more powerful than any spell keep me safe.

Khurahtaten comes to me less and less as I feel my own strength. Sometimes I long to ask him questions, but I soon learn that if the questions are important to me I will be given the answers — either in dream, or in conversation with someone I casually meet, or in some ancient papyrus I happen to be studying at the time. All I have to do is look around me with eyes to see. Everything and everyone is my mentor.

I am given a position of honour in the new temple, and take up residence there. One day Nefertiti and Merytaten come to the temple to see me. Merytaten runs to me at once, holding out her arms. I lift her in mine and swing her round. She laughs her lovely, bubbling, child's laugh and my heart sings. Young as she is, she is very like her mother.

Nefertiti looks at us both fondly.

"She insisted on coming to you today," she says.

Merytaten's arms are around my neck, her little face buried against my cheek. I can't stop smiling. I have family at last, love and the warmth of belonging. No one will take that away from me again. No one.

Nefertiti has changed in the past six years. The lithe, mischievous girl is gone. A woman who has borne, and is bearing, children is in her place — confident and poised. It is her strength that will make her husband's dream come true. Already I notice the sculptors are carving her image as large as her husband's, already she wears her crown with authority. I have seen strong men tremble when displeasure sparkles from her eyes. I have seen weak men become strong when she has smiled at them.

Today, her cheeks are glowing and her eyes shining.

"Can she stay here with you for a few days?" she asks.

Would any other temple in the land be asked to act as nursery to a five-year-old child? I remember my own childhood as the Oracle, the Nameless One, and shudder to think of any child exposed as I was to the long and tedious rituals, the gloom, the oppressive darkness. At Merytaten's age I was already cased in gold, and forced to sit statue-still from dawn to dusk, punished if I so much as moved a muscle or blinked an eye. In *this* temple she will run about and play in the sun's light, and at noon she will rest in a shaded garden.

"We are going to look at the site for our new city," Nefertiti says excitedly, and then, because she thinks I will be hurt not to have been asked to accompany them, she adds: "As soon as we are ready to put down the boundary stelae you will be called." I nod and smile, and swing the child around. What is a city to the mystery of the spirit that lives for ever! A city can be razed to the ground, and generations may walk unknowing on its dust, but a living being — ah, yes — a living being! Now, there is something worth thinking about. . . .

The new city is to be on a plain bounded by the river to the west, and a natural amphitheatre of limestone cliffs to the east. No city has ever been built there before — no temple, no palace. The powerful priests of Amun own not a grain of its sand, nor a sliver of its rock. It was a childhood dream of Amenhotep and Nefertiti to live in that place one day, having reunited there after a long separation, he returning south after years of study in the City of the Sun, and she sailing to meet him from her father's southern estates. Their two boats had come in sight of each other just as the sun partially emerged from cloud, casting long and brilliant rays to the earth, the fan-like shafts turning the bare plain to a magical, luminous gold. It had been one of those unforgettable moments, charged with emotion. They were a long, long way from the rigorous disciplines of the temple college at Lunu, and the rigidity of court ritual and protocol. They had picnicked there for a whole day and had never felt so happy. It was on that day that they knew they would be lovers.

In the third year of their marriage they had laid down three stelae marking the place, and had started planning and building. Now, in the sixth year, they will mark its boundaries more precisely with a further eleven stelae. They will ride in their chariot from point to point, followed by crowds of their people, marking their intentions in stone. He changes his name to Akhenaten: "the servant of Aten": names his city Akhetaten: "the horizon of the Aten": "the threshold from which the Eye of the Sun's Disk looks upon the world": and for Nefertiti he chooses the name: Nefer-nefru-aten: "fair is the goodness of Aten".

"Long live the Horus, Strong Bull, Beloved of Aten; the Two Ladies, Great in Sovereignty in Akhetaten; the Golden Horus, upholding the name of Aten; the King of Upper and Lower Egypt, Living in Truth, Lord of the Two Lands, Nefer-khepru-ré Wa'en-ré; the Son of the Sun, Living in Truth, Lord of Diadems, Akhenaten: Great in his length of days, who giveth life for ever and ever.

"The Hereditary Princess, Great of Favour, Mistress of Happiness, gay with the two feathers, at hearing whose voice one rejoices, soothing the heart of the King at home, pleased at all that is said, the Great and Beloved Wife of the King, Lady of the Two Lands, Nefer-nefru-aten Nefertiti living for ever.

"As my father the Aten lives, I will make Akhetaten for the Aten my father in this place. I will not make him Akhetaten south of it, north of it, west of it or east of it. And Akhetaten extends from the southern stele as far as the northern stele, measured between stele and stele on the eastern mountain, likewise from the south-west stele to the north-west stele on the western mountain of Akhetaten. And the area within these four stelae is Akhetaten itself: it belongs to Aten my father; mountains, deserts, meadows, islands, high ground and low ground, land, water, villages, men, beasts and all things which the Aten my father shall bring into existence eternally for ever. I will not neglect this oath which I have made to the Aten my father, eternally."

On an obelisk of red quartzite that sparkled in the rays of sun, Amenhotep inscribed a prayer from the ancient days to the sun-god, which for him had been the turning point in his long struggle to understand the gods. The words were not exceptional in themselves, but because they came to him at the moment when he was ready for them, they unlocked a door that for him would never close again:

May You wake in peace, O purified, in peace,
May You wake in peace, O Horus of the East, in peace,
May You wake in peace, O soul of the East, in peace,
May You sleep in the Night-bark,
May you wake in the Day-bark,
For You are He who oversees the gods,
There is no god who oversees You.

He causes this to be set up where the great temple to Aten is to be built.

For You are He who oversees the gods,
There is no god who oversees You.

How many times has the Spirit-from-whose-source-all-else-flows spoken: the words sounding in the minds of those who have ears to hear, like flute call or silver lute, but when translated into the language of time becoming like a drum crashing on the wrong beat, or a sistrum shaken to the wrong tune. Already I can see that my friend's clear and flowing vision will inevitably harden, as he is forced to flex his muscles against opposition; and as I look into the bright eyes of his children my seer's eye sees the shadows of the future, though as man I refuse to admit it.

The Temptation

The official move to the new city takes place two years after the boundary stelae are put down, and it reminds me of the great bird migrations I have witnessed, when countries to the north of us are touched by the cold, dark hands of winter. So many boats and barges have been requisitioned that the river must be groaning under their weight. Canopies flutter like bright wings about the royal party and their chosen priests, courtiers, craftsmen and the women of the harem. I am in the foremost boat, with the co-regent and his queen and their daughters. Merytaten, under the restraint of my arm, leans over the side to count the fishes, little Maketaten sitting on a high ebony stool beside us, asking no questions but staring at everything with greedy eyes as though she were seeing it for the last time. Ankhesenpaaten has the youngest daughter on her hip, and is walking her up and down the deck trying to quieten her cries. The baby is obviously frightened by the disturbance of her quiet routine and the crowds of strangers which, even on the royal boat, crowd round her. There is a feeling of tremendous excitement, as though this is the day of our birth, and we have been privileged to enjoy it with all the knowledge and awareness of being adult. I remember my journey to Waset, and how each thing I saw had opened my eyes a little further to the wonder and beauty of being alive. Now it is as though that in itself had been only a pale shadow to this new adventure, the richness of this new experience. I feel Merytaten move excitedly as she catches sight of the silver glint of scales under the blue-silver water, and I know that seeing things through her eyes, sharing them through our love for each other, is even better than I could ever have imagined or dreamed of in my lonely imprisoned years. How much else is there that I have not dreamed of?

Nefertiti comes close up beside us as her eldest daughter calls out her joy, the scent of the oils on her body stirring me. I try not to look at her, my heart filled with a desperate loyalty to my prince, but the beauty of Aten Himself could not outshine Nefertiti Nefer-nefru-aten, and when her cheek is so close to mine I can think of nothing else. Something in me resents Nefertiti, and something in me longs for her. Everything about her speaks of her love for her husband and yet — and yet she plays with me with her eyes, and her shoulder touches my arm unnecessarily as she leans over to kiss her daughter. I point out the fish which has already slid away from where Merytaten is pointing (or is it a totally different fish?); Nefertiti smiles, amused at the effect her closeness is obviously having on me, and mercifully moves away. I lift Maketaten to my shoulder and, holding Merytaten's hand, I take them both to the stern to see the canopies and the sails of the other boats, which stretch as far as the eye can see, a green island neatly dividing them, sacred ibises streaming away from them over the fields, white gulls flurrying and diving for scraps behind them.

My prince has arranged that we should arrive at noon, and the new city lies white in the heat, the air as thick as water, vibrating before our eyes. Canopies have been raised over the landing stages, and the co-regent's party, at least, is protected from the fiercest of the sun's rays while the proclamations of arrival are read, and my prince and I put the offerings we have brought on the new altar overlooking the river. Then, as we are carried to the Great Palace the other boats draw in to the quay, and bales and boxes and barrels are unloaded, overseers shout, servants complain, workmen on the half-finished buildings shout greetings and insults, whistling at the girls. Behind them come the people who have been chosen for the new city, the families who no doubt will become the aristocracy of the new order, the first families of Akhetaten, royal friends and their servants, and all the merchants, scribes, gardeners, brick-makers, stonemasons, tally-men and tax-collectors that will be needed to serve them.

I will live in the Great Temple, but my quarters are not yet completed. I am given a room in the palace overlooking the garden. Whole trees have been brought from the east and from Nubia, and channels have been dug from the river to water their roots and feed the lily ponds. I will be able to watch the lilies open as a free man. My heart rejoices at how unexpectedly life can turn about, and I am glad that I did not succeed in killing myself in the House of Many Thresholds.

During the last years of the old king's life my prince becomes more and more preoccupied with how he will reorganize the country under the new god. He has his father's blessing in this, though I suspect the old man doesn't realize quite how far his son intends to go. Amenhotep Nebma'atre' is not well. He is grossly over-weight, and has some infection of the gums that makes his life a misery. One by one he loses all his teeth, and banqueting, which used to be such a pleasure to him, becomes a nightmare. All the expert physicians are consulted, and when their methods fail to help, the medical papyrus that was such a marvel to King Khufu in the ancient days is brought out. But the king still suffers. When one of the Mitannian princesses comes to join his harem to cement relationships with her father, he requests that she bring with her the miracle-working statue of Ishtar from Nineveh, his own gods having failed to heal him. My prince is furious with him when he hears about this, and if his mother Tiye had not intervened, he would have smashed the famous idol to pieces, causing a very dangerous situation to develop. The Asian colonies of the Two Lands are restless enough without any further provocation.

As the old king becomes more and more disgruntled and miserable, Queen Tiye tries to interest him in the new city by bringing him, their infant son Tutankhaten, and their youngest daughter Baketaten, to watch the building, hoping that the bustle of activity and the gleaming new walls and tiles will remind him of the vigour of his youth when he himself broke away from Waset and built her a new palace at Per-hay well away from the city. She hopes the lake the young people are digging at Meru-Aten, to the south of their city, will remind him of the extraordinary feat he undertook when he dug her a lake in fourteen days, to comfort her because the priests of Amun had not given her the part of Amun's consort, Mut, in the great Opet festival. But his life is a burden to him, and not even his grandchildren can lighten his heart.

For those who have moved to Akhetaten, there is a feeling that all the world is fresh and new, and any dream is possible. Wherever you look beautiful new buildings stand proud. Even the poor quarters of the town are clean and well-constructed, with good drainage and ample room to breathe. Inscriptions everywhere are full of joy and praise, the concept of conquest and war apparently forgotten. The sculptors' studios ring with the sound of chisel and hammer, eager talk and laughter. The young artists rejoice in the freedom they have been given to break old rules and experiment with naturalism.

The royal family seem to be everywhere, easily accessible, full of enthusiasm for everything that is skilful and innovative. Even those portraits which are more like caricatures than genuine likenesses (and there are many before the sculptors master their new techniques) are passed by them, Nefertiti laughing heartily, Akhenaten telling himself that man-as-he-is is more precious to God than man-as-he-pretends-to-be. He is a little rueful sometimes when he gazes at some particularly uncompromising statue of himself, knowing that this is how posterity will see him, but the pleasure he feels at the liveliness of the work, and the fact that he is doing away with pretence and pretension, at last dispels the feeling.

I, with Merytaten at my side, am a familiar sight, she growing in stature and beauty with each new moon, I gradually unfolding like a flower in the warmth of her love. My feelings for Nefertiti become more and more ambiguous. I watch her manipulate her husband and know that it is her word that is law in the city, though Akhenaten thinks it is his. When she drives her chariot through the streets, her eyes sparkling, enjoying the speed and the feeling of the power of the reins in her hands, passers-by are honoured to be covered with the fine yellow dust from her wheels. She is an ambitious and a clever woman, but that is not necessarily a bad thing. Akhenaten the dreamer needs a partner with practical drive to implement his dreams, and when they are seen together hand in hand, arm in arm, cheek to cheek, their love is apparent to everyone. Is it jealousy then, I ask myself, that prevents my wholehearted acceptance of her? My friendship with Akhenaten is close, and it is she who always breaks up our long philosophical discussions. If this is jealousy, I am not sure whether it is because Akhenaten has Nefertiti, or because Nefertiti has Akhenaten.

But it is not only in the new city that temples are raised to Aten. Throughout the land, beside the old gods, Aten takes his stand: his altars open to the light, his cipher, the globe, with long rays reaching out to touch everything into life, with hands to bless the royal family, and through them all their subjects. On the whole requests for new temples for other gods are refused, and maintenance grants to existing temples cut. It is to pacify the growing concern of the powerful priests of Amun that Amenhotep Nebma'atre' orders a temple to Amun to be built in the south, but he knows, and they know, that this is not enough. When mysterious fires break out in the storerooms containing the precious oils and vestments in the new temple of Ra-Harakti (now dedicated fully to Aten) in Waset, I am sent to investigate.

This journey is not like the other. Then, at the first sight of the great and beautiful city my heart had raced to be part of it. But now it lies like a dark shadow on the land, the smell of fear in its temples, and a miasma of hate issuing from the minds of its priests. I had been relieved to leave it and I now dread to return. The sun shines as brightly here as on Akhetaten, but the quality of it seems different. It has a harshness, a cruelty. It is a breeder-of-flies-and-corruption rather than a giver-of-life-and-renewal.

As I disembark I fancy a group of men are watching me closely from behind some bales of linen-flax. They whisper, and one of their number glides away. I am greeted with eager courtesy by a deputation of young priests from the Temple of Aten. I can sense under their formal words a desperate holding-back, a sense of urgency that is made to take second place to protocol and politeness. I would relieve them of this was I not so aware of the watching eyes. Sacrilege had been committed in our temple, the fire had unmistakably been caused deliberately, and unthinkable blasphemous words had been scrawled on some of the walls. I must not let anyone see that we are worried or shaken. Calmly, I return the greeting, and calmly walk beside them through the streets, through the great portals of the temple complex, skirting Amun's sacred lake, white with geese, to the temple my prince has raised to the One God. Quietly I survey the damaged chambers, and see where the servants have washed out the offending words. Thoughtfully I look across at Amun's House. If Aten is seen to be humiliated with no redress, will He not lose His credibility with the people? How should I avenge His name? Time has already passed and Aten himself has not moved to punish those who have offended against Him. The priests of Amun will be laughing, preparing their next attack. My prince is anxious that no spells are used.

"The days of superstition and fear are over. The only magic in my kingdom will be the magic of life itself." It would be so easy to put a curse on them, I think, tempted. But if we want to clear out the dark side of magic from our land and free its people from the fear of it, *we* must not use it, no matter how tempted we are. From every deed a thousand spring; and every time we act we are responsible for the future.

My colleagues are now openly distressed, and interrupt each other to describe the horrors of the night of fire. I question them about every detail, hoping to be able to pin the act on someone specific who can be brought before the king's justice. There is no question in anyone's mind that the Amun priests are guilty, but they have been too clever for us. There is no evidence.

Someone has disturbed the geese on the lake, and the noise they make sounds like derisive laughter. My young colleagues look at me and each other, waiting for the noise to die down before they speak again. I wonder if the sound has chilled their blood as it has mine. Without our noticing their approach we have been joined by two priests of

Amun, one tall, the other short, both with faces like masks.

They express concern that we have suffered in this way, softly declaring that times are changing and respect for holy matters is not as it used to be.

I bow, but beg to disagree.

"There have always been vandals, tomb-robbers and heretics, and there have always been those who respect and honour the true and sacred mysteries." I look at them pointedly. "Both reap what they sow, whether it be in this world or the next."

It is their turn to bow. "True," they say piously. "Too true," but they betray not the slightest flicker of guilt. And then they deliver an invitation from Na-aghta. My heart sinks. I dread meeting him again. I tell myself it will be different this time. This time I am strong and free, I have the co-regent of the Two Lands as my friend. This time they can do nothing to me. But all the horrors of my early years return, and I shiver. The tall priest of Amun notices this and for a moment his mask-like expression slips, and I see a snake glint in his eyes. Ah, Aten, Mother-Father of us all, give me strength in this confrontation.

They bow again and leave. My young priests, who have been silent and outraged throughout this exchange, begin to talk, too fast, and all at once.

The invitation is for today. I have had a night's sleep since I arrived in Thebes — or shall I say a night has passed in tossing and turning and praying — and now it is the dawn. I perform the rituals at the rising of the sun, feeling strength and confidence growing with each incantation:

"*You who oversee the gods, whom no god oversees: help me.*
You who were before all things and will be beyond all things:
  help me.
You who understand all that there is, there being nothing
  beyond your understanding: help me.

Light of the Overworld. Light of all the Thresholds. Light of
our sleeping and our waking: help me. . . ."

I set off for the Temple of Amun confident in my god.

Na-aghta is no fool. He does not meet me in the first
court, nor the second. He has his tall messenger lead me
through court after court, hall after hall. There is no sign of
another living man. I already feel small compared to the
man who accompanies me. Once among the columns I
shrink further at each step. I suspect I am not being taken
directly to him, but am being led back and forth among the
colonnades and through the tallest, darkest chambers, so
that I will lose my bearings. The hugeness and darkness is
oppressive, the shafts of light from the clerestory windows
serving only to enhance the contrast with the shadows.
There is a dreadful silence apart from our own footsteps.
Occasionally I think I hear someone behind us, but when I
turn to look there is no one there. It could be the echo, or it
could be that there is someone following us who keeps out
of sight. Where are all the people who normally serve the
temple, the lithe dancers and singers, the priests and
novices, the scribes, the cleaners, the cooks, the tithe
collectors and administrators? The whole place seems
deserted — yet I sense a dark and brooding presence.

We reach a door at last and my silent companion knocks
with his staff three times. The door creaks when it opens,
and I am waved before him into a chamber only dimly lit
with tapers. It must be deep in the building and has no
means of admitting natural light. Na-aghta is there. Huge
reliefs of the triad, Amun, his consort Mut and their son
Khonsu, are carved on the walls behind him. The taper
light flickers, and his shadow moves grotesquely over
them. He has succeeded in frightening me. A pulse beats in
my neck so insistently I am surprised he doesn't see it and
comment on it. I hear the door shut behind me, and all the
terrors of my childhood return. Sweat begins to run down

65

my face and body, part of it due to the close, suffocating heat of the room, part to my fear. But I have learned something in my years of freedom and keep my head held high, meeting his eyes boldly. He is standing, and he is taller than I am.

"My Lord Priest, Prophet of Amun," I say, forcing my voice to be steady, "I am grateful for your courtesy in inviting me here. I presume it is for the purpose of offering an explanation and an apology for what happened at the Temple of Aten-Lord-of-all-Horizons." Something of my courage has returned as I remember the prayers I had fortified myself with before I set off.

His expression is coldly amused.

"My Lord Priest, Prophet of Aten, I assure you I have no explanation for anything that happens in your precinct. If your inferiors are careless, that is a matter surely that has to be dealt with within your own temple."

I am silent, but meet his eyes steadily. I remember how Ma-nan used to control me, and am wary.

"I have invited you here," he says smoothly, "because I think it is time we discussed matters to our mutual advantage."

"You mean the rule of Maat, the felicity of the rule of Wisdom and Justice in our country," I say equally smoothly.

He bites his lip very slightly and I think, perhaps, I have surprised him.

"Of course," he says with a shade of impatience, and I feel I have the edge on him for the moment. "It has not escaped our notice," he continues, recovering his composure, "that our royal co-regent Amenhotep —"

"Akhenaten," I correct him pointedly.

"Akhenaten," he acknowledges with a slight twist of his mouth," is giving increasing support to this minor god —"

"We speak of no minor god," I say quietly. "The God Aten has existed before and will exist after. It is He who spoke in the great void and it is His eye that is the consciousness of all things."

Na-aghta's eyes flash.

"These things are claimed for our Father Amun. It is Amun who is the Creator of all things."

"His coffers fill while the bellies of his people empty. Is that the sign of the Father?"

"My lord, take care," he says; and his voice is as hard and sharp as the cutting edge of a sword. Behind him I sense something move. In the dim light I strain my eyes. A shadow detaches itself from the other shadows and a figure joins the high priest.

It is Ma-nan.

It seems to me all the blood drains out of my face, and I clench my fists to prevent my hands shaking. He looks at me, up and down, for what seems an eternity. My throat is constricted and, try as I will, I can bring out no words.

"Greeting, Nameless One," he says mockingly, noting my discomfiture. For a moment I almost fall under the old spell. I have not called on Khurahtaten for help for a long time, but I call now. I know I have not the strength even yet to stand against the man who caged me all those years.

A voice speaks softly behind my back, though there is no one there. "You have names reaching back to the Beginning. Have courage."

"I am named Sothis," I say, and this time my voice leaves my throat and fills the dark chamber powerfully. "You have no more power over me."

"Was Sothis the name your mother cried at your birth?"

"No. It is the name my king has given me."

"What words did your mother cry?"

"You know as well as I, I do not know my mother."

"Nor your father?" The tone of his voice shows me that these are not idle questions. He is leading to something.

"Nor my father," I say, my heart pounding. Is this the moment? Is it now I will learn the names of my mother and my father? Is it now my life is to be placed in history — to

67

have a before and an after that men will record?

There is a terrible silence in the chamber as the two men stare at me, and I hold back the questions that I ache to ask.

"I could give you the names of your mother and your father," Ma-nan says at last, very, very slowly.

I say nothing.

Khurahtaten my friend, help me! What is it to know the names of your mother and your father? He will not give them to me for nothing. *Fall not into his trap . . . fall not . . . fall not. . . .* I know it is Khurahtaten's voice urging the caution in my ears.

"I don't wish to know them," I say at last, and all the pain of my childhood wells up in my heart. I begin to tremble uncontrollably, tears pouring from my eyes. Through them I see the triumph in the eyes of the two men before me. They know what it has cost me to say what I have said, and they smile.

I turn and stumble from the room. I wait for no one to usher me through the labyrinth of passages. I am staggering like a drunken man as I hurry away from my tormentors. They know — and they know *I* know — that they have me trapped. I'll not have a moment's peace now until I have the names of my mother and my father.

I hear footsteps behind me and I start to run. I feel that I cannot bear to face anyone. I see a door, and with a desperate burst of energy I fling myself at it, and drag it open. Then I slam the door shut behind me and stand panting heavily, leaning against the heavy wood. I turn my right ear to the timber, and strain to catch any sound made by my pursuers. My heart is beating so loudly at one point it is difficult to tell whether the sounds I hear are the thud of footsteps outside in the corridor, or the drumming of my own heart.

I have no idea into which chamber I have stumbled.

It seems to me at last that both the excessive beating of my heart and the noises in the corridor have died down. I

glance round to take my bearings and suddenly freeze —
the hairs on the back of my neck rising.

By the flickering light of torches I see that I am in the
sanctuary of Sekhmet. Towering above me is the huge
black basalt statue of the goddess with the watchful head of
a lioness and the body of a woman. She is seated, and in her
one hand she holds the ankh, the sign of life, and in the
other the rod of her divinity: but it is her eyes that terrify
me. I feel her presence. The statue is alive with her. She is
looking directly at me with the wary, totally absorbed stare
of a lion watching its prey.

I back against the door and fumble at the catch. To my
horror, I find that the door is now locked and I cannot get
out. Whether the catch snapped back as I slammed it shut,
or whether someone locked it from the outside once I was
in — either knowing that I was inside or unaware of it — I
can't say; but I am trapped in a chamber almost entirely
filled by the fearsome goddess whose rage nearly destroyed
mankind, whose hot breath blows the desert storms, and
who has the power to tear down mountains and devastate
cities. I press my back hard against the solid wooden door,
as far away as I can get. The statue appears totally still and
calm, yet I can sense the powerful energy of her — the
tension of a great cat poised for the kill.

At first I am too frightened to think, my body running
with sweat. The chamber, apart from anything else, is
unbearably, suffocatingly hot. I try to bring myself under
control. My king has taught me that there is only the One,
the Aten. If so, she, the Great Destroyer, is but the fierce
and violent instrument of his anger. I ask myself if I have
reason to believe that I have drawn that anger down
upon myself, and I know I cannot answer truthfully that I
have not.

I begin to edge around the huge plinth on which she
rests, hoping against hope that there might be a small door
at the back of the sanctuary. Sometimes there is one for the

oracle to enter, but not often. The space between the wall and the side of the goddess is so narrow, and I am so clumsy with nervousness, that I inadvertently touch her foot as I squeeze past. For a moment all the breath is knocked from my body and a blinding pain shoots through me. Gasping, I fall back, and it seems to me as though lightning is playing about her form, crackling in jagged rays from her fingertips, clothing her in an ever-changing aura of fierce and rippling light.

I fall to my knees and find myself gibbering with fear, pleading with the gods, any and every one. The words come out jumbled; tumbling like discarded trinkets from a dusty box, but from behind them something is trying to get through to me — the Nameless One, the First, The Only True One. . . . Suddenly I know to whom I should be praying, to whom I should be calling out.

The light around her fades and the menacing blackness of the stone from which her image is carved returns.

I stand up. I look into her eyes. I cease to fear. I cease to tremble.

She looks back calmly into my eyes. She is no less magnificent, no less powerful and real, but now I see another aspect of her: the Protector; the fierce Defender. It is no accident that in the ancient teaching of Men-Nefer her husband is Ptah, the craftsman, the creator, he who fashioned the ten million things of this earth upon his potter's wheel. It is no accident that from this union of the Creator and the Destroyer, Nefer-tum was born, rising from the lotus. The teaching tells how this child, poised between the two, pulled from either side by energies too great to bear, wept, and from his tears mankind was born. The destruction she brings is never wanton, never random. She and her husband Ptah together create and destroy matter for ever, the balance between the two necessary for existence. If the balance is upset — and man can do it if he chooses — then only are her powers dangerous and inimical.

I respect her. I stand before her in awe, meeting her strength eye to eye. No longer afraid.

"Hail, Sekhmet, lady of the gods, who holdeth her fan of the lady of the scarlet garment, the mistress of the white and red crown; the great magician in the boat of millions of years, lofty when she rises in the abode of silence; the royal wife of the lion; the mother on the horizon of the sky, the joyful, the beloved, who destroyeth the rebels collected in her fist. . . . Hail!"

It is she who tells me to try the locked door again. I know before I touch it that it will now open — and it does.

As I leave the temple of Amun the sunlight smashes into my face and almost blinds me.

Rumours reach us at Akhetaten that the priests of Amun are working with spells to destroy us. A series of accidents in the city make the superstitious very nervous, but Akhenaten goes from place to place, calling the people to him, speaking like a father, telling them that spells can have no effect against the strength of the Aten.

"Think of our city surrounded by a high invisible wall with every gate guarded. Inside the city there are gardens and pleasant homes, people living at peace and in joy. Is this not how it is, my people?" he calls out, suddenly raising his voice. The answer is immediate and enthusiastic. There are indeed pleasant homes and many gardens in Akhetaten, and people living peacefully.

"This is how it is, our father, our King!"

"In such a city, enclosed by such walls, no enemy can reach us."

The people cheer.

"*But* — " he adds warningly, and the people are silent as he lowers his voice, making it deep and sombre — "but if someone opens the gate, then may the forces of our enemy enter and destroy us."

There is a murmur of fear.

"The walls of our faith may be invisible — but they are strong. The gates of our faith may be impregnable — but if a traitor opens them, we are lost."

He looks down at the faces of his people.

"Who is the traitor who will do this, my people?"

No one answers. They look uneasily at each other. What does he mean?

"Doubt is the traitor!" he shouts. *"Fear is the traitor!"*

The people sigh and groan and go away to their homes determined to be strong and steadfast in their faith.

But — of course — that is not as easy as it sounds.

Later in the year, the princess Maketaten becomes gravely ill, and there is no doubt in many minds that it is the work of the hostile spells from the Amun priests. Physicians from the famous college at Lunu are called to her side.

When they fail to help her, her father and I as priests of the Aten try what the priests of Hathor have tried from ancient times. We lay her on the couch in the chamber of dreams and leave her alone and in silence with the lamps of the going-out and the coming-in, of the wishing and of the dreading. Through a hole in the wall we watch as she gradually falls asleep, becoming one with the great ocean that was before all things. We see the pain on her thin face as she turns from side to side, as though to break free of the wings of Horus that hold her to the head-rest. Then the fighting stops; and gradually the Peace of the Great One that is beyond all understanding enfolds her, and she sleeps as all things slept in the heart of God before the separation into this and that, here and there, then and now.

All night we keep vigil from outside the chamber, monitoring every movement of her eyelids, every twitch of her limbs, praying that we will be given wisdom at the time of interpretation. In the morning more lamps are lit, the lamps of the waking and the remembering, and her father and I move in and sit beside her, speaking the words of asking in the manner prescribed by the ancient texts.

Before she wakes she answers us, words floating to the surface of her mind and drifting off like smoke. We have to register them quickly before, like smoke, they fade and disappear. The interpretation of her dreams is given us by our god in answer to our prayers. She sees herself as a cormorant tied by a thread to the wrist of a fisherman . . . longing to be free. She sees herself as the fish caught in its beak . . . longing to be free. She sees herself as the fisherman taking the fish from the bird's beak, held himself by a thread to the shadowy figure of hunger behind him — he, too, longing to be free.

"You are free," whispers Akhenaten, leaning close to her, his tears falling on her soft, pale cheek. "You are the king's daughter . . . beloved of Aten . . . you are free. . . ."

She sighs, and opens her eyes.

She looks at us deeply puzzled, as though we are strangers, and then she reaches out her arms to someone we cannot see, and her face lights up in recognition.

It is then we know that she is ready to leave us and there is nothing we can do about it.

The flower city of Akhetaten becomes a place of weeping. There is not a man, woman or child who has seen the princess since she came to live in the horizon of the globe, and has not thought her lovely.

Merytaten is inconsolable and turns to me for comfort, but I desert her and leave for Waset. I tell myself Maketaten's death is Na-aghta's doing, that he has induced her dreams and led her away from us: but deep inside I know that this is nonsense, that the child has been ailing since birth and was never intended to wear the cloak of this life for long. I tell myself the lie because I want an excuse to confront Na-aghta and Ma-nan.

Without invitation I storm through the complex of buildings that surrounds the sanctuary of Amun, stride through the echoing corridors, and halls misty with the smoke of incense. I surprise a group of slender temple-dancers at their practice and cause the musicians to falter. Archivists walking from one chamber to another with papyrus rolls fall back staring, one dropping a long roll that unravels in front of me like a carpet. Novices call after me. At last my way is barred by the same tall man with the staff who had led me such a devious route before.

"I demand to see Na-aghta," I say boldly, knowing that I am insulting him by not giving him his full title. I am hot with determination, my only fear that I will be forced to wait somewhere and have time to cool down.

"Demand?" he says coldly.

My anger makes me think I have courage.

"Demand!" I reply fiercely.

He stares at me balefully for a long moment or two and then nods, turns and leads the way.

Na-aghta is busy in the store-house berating the master of granaries. The man is trying to explain that it is the fault of the co-regent that the place is not as full as it should be, and stops in mid-sentence, embarrassed when he sees me. Na-aghta turns to see who it is, and looks momentarily astonished. But only momentarily.

"This man," my guide says scornfully, and I notice he uses none of my titles, "demands to see you, my lord Priest, honoured Prophet, Beloved of Amun."

Na-aghta has already composed himself.

"Greetings, Priest of Aten." His intonation is insulting.

I flush, but say nothing. I am still holding carefully to my anger. He looks at my red face with amusement. I am half aware that the master of the granaries is thankfully sliding away. My guide is gripping his staff like a weapon, ready to defend his master, physically if need be.

"Have your unruly followers been setting your store-rooms on fire again?" Na-aghta asks with mock solicitude.

Suddenly it seems to me crazy to accuse him of killing the princess Maketaten. It had seemed so plausible when everyone was murmuring around me. Now my good sense returns to me, and leaves me washed up like a fish on dry land. What am I to accuse him of? What demand? I know what I want — but I cannot say it.

He is a man of great subtlety: a formidable opponent. He knows why I have come. Smiling, he indicates that I should follow him. I do so. The arrogance with which I had entered the building is leaving me, and my stride becomes less sure, my back less straight. I am taken to an inner chamber and told to wait.

I sit on a leather and ebony chair and wonder why I have been such a fool. But gradually, as the confusion of my thoughts settles, I know that I was right to come. Whether he caused the death of Maketaten or not is not the issue. The issue is that he is still powerful enough to inspire fear, and make people believe he is capable of killing a royal princess in the safety of her home many leagues away. I know that Nefertiti herself believes it, though her husband strives to dissuade her. Of late it has worried me a little that she seems to be dabbling herself, privately, in spells.

I know that I will ask Na-aghta, and Ma-nan if he appears, who my father and my mother are. The question has been tormenting me, as they knew it would, ever since the day I learnt that they could tell me. I reason that I am becoming useless to my prince because I am so preoccupied with this question. My sleep is suffering, and so is my health. I can settle to nothing. As a child it had haunted me continually, but since I have gained my freedom, and my name, it has hardly crossed my surface-mind. Bitterly I resent their raising of this old ghost.

Na-aghta returns — with Ma-nan. I stand at once, and bow politely to him. Long years of hate are held in check. I want to know — I need to know — what only he can tell me. When I have the information I will concentrate on out-witting them for my prince. I know that Ma-nan is illegally in the country. Na-aghta could well be arrested for harbouring him.

The two men stand before me and we wait, each for the other to make the first move.

It is I, the fool, who speak first.

"You told me that you had certain information for me." The two men look at each other and smile, and look back at me. "If that is still the case, I am now prepared to listen," I say.

Ma-nan prowls like a restless lion, circling me, looking at me.

"You are a man now," he says with deadly sweetness. "You are the friend of kings. Do you remember how I nurtured you as an infant, cared for you as a child?"

"I will never forget," I say grimly.

"You repaid me with ingratitude," he says silkily.

"I admit I have never repaid you as you deserved," I reply, pleased with the ambiguity.

Na-aghta is enjoying the game, but keeps out of it.

"Why should I do you a favour?" Ma-nan purrs.

"You offered — I did not ask."

"You are asking now."

I wonder if I can walk out — not knowing — once again; and I know that I cannot. He knows that I cannot. He waits for me to ask what I should offer him in return, but I manage to hold my tongue. At last he grows impatient.

"I miss my own country. I miss the Two Lands," he says.

"You are in your own country. You are in the Two Lands," I say.

"You know I cannot walk freely in the streets. You know I cannot sail on the river."

"It is not in my power to take off the sentence of banishment," I say. "But it is in my power to report that you have broken the king's command." Perhaps I can blackmail him into telling me what I need to know.

"The heretic's command," Na-aghta says suddenly,

turning the game about.

I look at him, shocked.

"That is treason," I say sharply. I know I should rush straight out of the temple, call the king's guards and have these men arrested before I become any more involved. My prince would thank me for it. He is looking for an excuse to crush the prestige of the priests of Amun. But a maggot is beginning to gnaw at my heart. A maggot that, if not killed, could devour my whole body. The two men know it is there, and play with me.

"What will you do for me if I tell you who you are?"

I am silent. I am in agony.

"I want to return to my country as a free man."

"That may be possible to arrange," I hear myself saying. I think I sense Khurahtaten in the room but I refuse to look at him — refuse to listen to him.

"Amun must have the lands diverted from him to Aten returned. Aten must be declared subsidiary to Amun."

"That is not possible." My voice betrays my disappointment. Akhenaten will never agree to this. I am lost. Years of torturing curiosity await me.

They look at each other, and I can see that they are considering whether they haven't perhaps demanded too much as a first step. Na-aghta nods almost imperceptibly at Ma-nan. Khurahtaten is shouting in my ears, but I will not listen. I am sweating. *Go away!* I cry in my head. *Go away! I don't need you. I know what I am doing!*

"You think the co-regent will not agree to our terms?" Na-aghta asks smoothly.

"I know he won't," I say miserably, hopelessly enmeshed now, and not even trying to win the game.

"But if he is no longer the co-regent? If he does not become king?"

How could I have fallen once again into the clutches of Ma-nan? I remember Akhenaten's words about the traitor who opens the gate, and inside I am weeping. I have never

77

been greedy or ambitious — why now? Why now? Khurah-taten, is it too late? But he has gone. I am on my own.

"Tell me who my parents are," I demand, a terrible conviction that I already know growing within me. But whatever the answer I know I have already gone too far to turn back.

Ma-nan smiles and closes his trap.

"Your father is the Pharaoh Amenhotep Nebma'atre', the beloved son of Amun, the father of all gods. Your mother is his wife-daughter, Sitamon."

It is said.

There is a long and terrible silence as the two men study my reactions.

"You lie!" I say at last in a dry, dry voice. "If I were the son of the king and his daughter. . . ."

The silence in the chamber becomes painful.

If? But why — why, if this is so, am I not living like a prince . . .? Am I not the co-regent myself? Sitamon's blood is of the royal line: as eldest daughter of the king she is the royal heiress. I have seen portraits of her as God's Wife of Amun, the wings of Mut's vulture head-dress close about her ears. Tiye's blood is common, even though her husband's love has given her the title of First and Great Royal Wife, and her son is declared his heir. I remember Tiye's eyes — the way she looks at me. It is because of *her* I have been denied. It is because of *her* I was given no name, hidden like an unclean thing.

"Tell me . . ." I say brokenly, humbly, to my old enemy.

He smiles.

"Need I tell you? You are no fool. You know the ambition of the queen for her own flesh and blood."

"But — " I was thinking of Sitamon herself. Was she so over-awed by Tiye that she allowed herself to be taken as wife then kept in obscurity among the foreign princesses as though she were no more than they? Childless as far as anyone knew; dying young. I had never seen her, except

78

perhaps in a dream, weeping, standing behind her father-husband and his wife, Tiye.

Somewhere in my heart words I can hardly comprehend are beating. *Akhenaten is my brother! Akhenaten is my brother!*

It seems to me that the great void is very, very near. I could reach out and pick up the crook and the flail — or I could reach out and pick up a festering bag of maggots.

"*Enough*," I say sharply. "Your story is preposterous."

I turn on my heel and stride out of the room. Instinct must have shown me the way through the labyrinth of corridors, because I am almost blind with tears. Only once a sound makes me turn my head and, through an open doorway, I see the old king's favourite general, Horemheb, the one whom Akhenaten feared and respected so much in his youth.

Little Maketaten is hardly in her tomb when we receive news that Akhenaten's father (*my* father!) is seriously ill, and not expected to live more than a few days. Events are happening too fast. I have not had time to work out exactly what I am going to do about the information I now carry like a great lead weight about my neck. I have told no one as yet and hope that I will have the strength never to tell anyone.

When the call comes for Akhenaten to visit the deathbed of his father, the request comes for me to accompany him.

"I always remember," Akhenaten says thoughtfully, "how angry he was when I asked after you that time we saw you at Men-Nefer when you were still an oracle."

My heart beats faster. Is my relationship going to be made known at last without my having to declare it myself? I pray that it is. The secret I am keeping is almost destroying me, as Ma-nan knew it would. *How cunning they are*, I think. If I take the bait I will reinstate Amun in gratitude to them. If I do not, I will still never have another moment's peace of mind, and my friendship with

Akhenaten, the friendship on which he has grown to depend so heavily, will be changed and soured. Nefertiti has noticed the change in me already, and has asked me on several occasions what the matter is. Each time I deny that there is anything. Each time she has looked less convinced.

Since my return from Waset, Merytaten has been estranged from me. I know it is because I deserted her when she needed me after the death of her younger sister, but I am in no mood to be subtle and tender. I am moody and awkward and keep myself to myself, until it is she who seeks me out and, putting her arms around my neck, pleads with me to forgive her, although it is I who have been at fault. We cling together, and in that clinging I vow that whether I tell of my royal birth or not, I will have Merytaten to wife — though how this will be possible for a "commoner" I do not know.

We all go to Per-hay. Akhenaten and Nefertiti, their daughters (only five now, since Maketaten's death), and Akhenaten's little brother Tutankhaten, and sister Baketaten, who had been left in the new city while the queen attended her ailing husband.

I have not been in the king's private chambers before and am impressed, if a little disturbed, by the heavy opulence around me. Our city is light and bright and sparkling. His room is painted crimson and gold, the furniture black ebony, the screens the same. The statue of Ishtar that he had borrowed from Nineveh dominates one side of the room. Some say that Ishtar is just another name for our Isis; but I must say I find her presence in this place alien and oppressive. She has been no help to our king, though in her own land she is famous for the miracles she has wrought. I ponder on this. Taking over a divinity from another people, without understanding how her very being is dependent on the deepest thoughts and aspirations of her people, is like taking a palm tree to a cold climate, and expecting it to grow. Her life's blood is the active belief of her people. Here the king is believing in her at one remove, as it were. He has heard she has wrought miracles — but his heart does not know it as her people know it. Thinking about this makes me wonder if Akhenaten will be able to change the beliefs of his people overnight as he hopes. He has not taken into account the fact that belief has a life of its own, and that the energy generated in this way is powerful in itself whether the object of the belief is genuine or not. How much more powerful, I think, awed, would a belief be if it were grounded on truth! With such a belief a man could raise the dead or walk on water.

Queen Tiye, her face red and swollen with weeping, and her brother Ay, the king's close friend, adviser and master of horse, sit on either side of his bed.

Amenhotep Nebma'atre', the great king who has ruled the Two Lands for nearly forty years, is barely conscious. I think of the statues I have seen of him, the beautiful young man in full vigour, carved in stone that will endure for ever. He was handsome when I first saw him, though thicker in the waist even then than the sculptors made him. Now he is an ugly hump of flesh in the bed, his breath rasping, his festering mouth dribbling. But Tiye sees him as he was, a lover tender and fiery, a good-humoured ruler, enjoying fine things.

We gather round the bed, directed by the thin sharp finger of the chief physician. I hear a disturbance at the door and Horemheb strides in. The physician protests and tries to wave him back. Tiye looks up sharply and indicates that Horemheb may stay.

The chamber is hot and crowded. The flies are already gathering, the servants swishing at them with ostrich-feather fans. Little Tutankhaten looks as though he is going to be sick and Tiye, ever in command, indicates to Ay's wife Tey, Nefertiti's step-mother, that the smaller children should be removed. There is bustle and noise for a moment as they are ushered out. I hear Tutankhaten throwing up in the antechamber and slip my hand into Merytaten's. Her face is very white and her hand is trembling. She is still a child, but is expected to behave like a grown woman.

It looks as though the disturbance has penetrated the old king's coma. His eyelids flutter and Tiye leans forward eagerly. Without looking up, Tiye crooks a finger at Akhenaten, and he moves forward to lean beside her and to stare into his father's face. They have not been close — the son competing always with his dead brother for his father's affection. In a sense, Akhenaten has been impatient for this moment, anxious to go further with the installation of Aten as sole god than his father would allow him; but there are things for which he will regret his passing. Horemheb pushes himself forward and whispers something in the king's ear. The sick old man opens his eyes and gazes round himself, bewildered, as though looking for someone. His eye falls on me and stops there. Horemheb whispers again, and Tiye tells him sharply to be quiet and move back. As he reluctantly moves back he looks hard at me. Nefertiti has not missed a thing. Tiye puts her firm brown hand on her husband's chin and turns his head so that his eyes meet those of Akhenaten. The co-regent, guided by Tiye's other hand, leans forward and kisses his father's forehead.

I am at a loss to know what to do. Horemheb is willing me to step forward and make myself known to my father. I can feel it. But my loyalty to Akhenaten is too strong, and I am resisting. Merytaten leans her head against my arm, and for a moment a longing to be acknowledged as a royal prince, and therefore acceptable as a husband for Merytaten, overwhelms me. I forget what it will do to Akhenaten. I take a step forward. Nefertiti moves as silently as a cat and cuts off my path to the king. I see the dark and furious look Horemheb gives her, and know

82

that he is not an enemy I would like to have.

The king is dead, and I have not been declared his son.

I too look at Nefertiti; my eyes for the moment filled with hate.

For the next seventy days while the old king's body is being embalmed, the country is officially in mourning, but behind the scenes the preparations for the regent's coronation as full pharaoh go ahead. Everyone has his or her part to play in both the funeral and the coronation, and there is hardly a moment when I leave my prince's side. He seems to be relying on me more than ever to support him in his plans, and I haven't the heart to let a hint of what has been going on in my mind disturb him. If the old king had declared for me.... But as he did not, I decide to keep silent: determined that my secret will go with me to my death.

Tiye, always the power behind the throne, is still in charge. She insists that her son marry one of his own daughters to make sure there is no question of doubt about his accession to the throne. Nefertiti, like herself, is not a fully legitimate female heir, and she knows that Horemheb, in a powerful position as head of the army, has objections to Akhenaten's accession because of his enmity towards the army's god, Amun. I am terrified that Akhenaten will choose Merytaten, his eldest daughter, and I spend a night in the desert battling with myself, the star Sothis witness to my suffering. Horemheb has tried to see me several times, but each time has been prevented either by my own evasive tactics or by Nefertiti. I cannot make out whether Nefertiti knows what she is doing, or is acting blindly, from instinct.

Akhenaten chooses his third daughter, Ankhesenpaaten, and I find Merytaten weeping in the garden with relief. We kiss as lovers kiss, and both know that we cannot live without each other. She begs me to ask her father if she can be my wife, but I tell her the time is not right. There is the

funeral to get through and the coronation. Then, perhaps
. . . when things have settled down. To ask and be refused
— that I couldn't bear. She can't see that refusal is a strong
possibility. Nor can she know the turmoil I am in. At one
moment I tell myself how sweet it would be to be pharaoh:
the next I remember what the cost to my brother would be.
I have no longing for worldly power as some men have,
and am content to work in the spirit for the renaissance of
the spirit.

Horemheb is sent by Akhenaten on the advice of Nefertiti
to the frontier, where the vassal countries, knowing that
the old king is dead, try their strength. Within a short while
of his presence there letters begin to come, offering loyalty
to the new pharaoh but demanding expensive favours in
return. Over the past few years hundreds of letters have
been received, requesting help, complaining of help not
given. All are filed away carefully in the archives at
Akhetaten. These new letters are also filed. My brother
believes that the frontier states will settle down as soon as
Horemheb has explained that the double crown of the Two
Lands is in safe hands and that the Aten, the great circle of
Divine Light, encompasses them all.

He has never liked Horemheb, but respects him as his
father's favourite and most trusted general, and would
have invited him home for the funeral had Nefertiti not
persuaded him otherwise. The young queen seems under a
great strain and has lost much of her kittenish enthusiasm
for life. Her face at times is quite drawn, as though she has
had very little sleep, and she frequently treats me with
coldness. I find myself beginning to fear her, though
sometimes I wonder if I am not doing her an injustice. If she
loves her husband and is loyal to him, it would be natural
for her to be wary of anyone she believed to be a threat to
him. I don't know how she could possibly know of the
matters Na-aghta and Ma-nan had discussed with me —

but it seems she does. Perhaps it is just shrewd observation. Or perhaps. . . . I suddenly start and all the colour drains from my face. Perhaps she and Horemheb . . .? Never! If anything, she hates Horemheb. Has she not persuaded her husband to leave him at the frontier, so that he will miss the funeral and the inevitable manoeuvring for power that will accompany it? The other possibility is Tiye. She certainly knows who I am, and she might well have told her favourite niece and daughter-in-law, so that they could work together to protect Akhenaten from the threat they believe I pose.

After his coronation Akhenaten wastes no time in making public pronouncements that the mystery of the One God is to be represented by the disk of the sun and by no other image. All other images representing the manifold aspects of the One God, which have formerly been called "gods" and have been worshipped as such, are to be recognized as secondary attributes of the One God, which they always were, and nothing more. Any priest who claims otherwise is to be deprived of his office; and if he further persists in his folly he is to be outlawed, and declared nameless. Swiftly, the king's soldiers fall upon the priests of Amun-Ra at Ipet-Esut, and expel by force all who are within the temple precincts. Workmen are deputed throughout the land to hack out all references to Amun as the supreme deity, and to substitute images of the new pharaoh, his queen and their symbol of the Aten, the sun's disk with its rays ending in hands holding the ankh, the symbol of eternal life, above their heads. Mighty Waset, deserted by the rich and powerful families who had followed Akhenaten to his new capital, becomes a quiet backwater. Dispersed throughout the Two Lands her disaffected priests find niches for themselves, biding their time.

My dreams at night are often disturbed by dark images: Ma-nan's familiars, howling round my bed, he himself with eyes as blank as jet, standing in the doorway offering me the two crowns. Many a night I stand up and pace the room to escape my dreams, asking myself what I would do if I were king. My gentle admonitions have increasingly little effect on my friend and brother. He cannot see that under the surface of the victorious edifice that he has built for Aten, the ground is not firm, and the slightest pressure from a determined enemy could bring it tumbling down. Because men smile and bow, and obey his commands, he believes they understand and accept his teaching. Many a time I visit the house of a labourer as a healer-priest, and find small effigies and talismans of the traditional gods that have been hastily and inexpertly hidden at my approach. I never report this to the king, because I find lately that he tends to punish such lapses. His dream of freeing his country from fear by bathing it in the light of truth has not taken into account two things: one, the natural tendency of humans to hold to old, familiar ideas as firmly as an infant holds to its cot cover; and two, the corrupting influence of power. He does not seem to notice that by the suddenness of his new decrees and the warnings he issues at any breach of them, he has not rid his people of fear, only changed the source of it. But perhaps I am being too critical. Certainly in his city of Akhetaten there are very few shadows. What is happening in the rest of the country, as his officers enforce his new laws, we do not know, but in Akhetaten we live in a golden age. All that is beautiful is encouraged: art, singing, music, dancing; festivals celebrating each year of the new king's reign; festivals of rejoicing at each of the royal birthdays. Breaking once again with tradition, tombs are started for the royal family and high officials, in the mountains to the east of the city — where the sun rises. Death is to be a journey of the day — not of the night.

I am sitting in the shade of a sycamore tree in the garden of my house. It is noon, and the city is sleeping. Even the dog, lying under the lee of the wall, is too lethargic to do more than open one eye and cock an ear as a figure walks softly past him. When he sees who it is his tail wags momentarily and then falls back on to the warm flagstones again.

I know her step, but pretend I have heard nothing. Soon her soft hands are over my eyes and I can feel the curves of her body on my back. I lean my head against her breasts. She kisses the top of my head but still keeps her hands firmly over my eyes. I know I am supposed to guess who she is and I go through all the names of her sisters. And then I start on other names, as though I have had many lovers. She drops her hands angrily — but before she can move away I twist about to take her by the shoulders, and swing her round till she is close against my chest and my lips can reach hers. After her lips I kiss her eyelids and her ears.

She jerks her ear-lobe away and I see the marks of my teeth still on the flesh.

"Who are these other women?" she asks sharply.

"Are you not my only love?" I ask, and, by trying to keep my tone light, I make it mocking. I regret it at once. I have stupidly spoiled a beautiful moment.

She is flushed, angry. She starts to move away. I take her arm more roughly than I intend to pull her back to me.

"Let me go," she says fiercely.

"No," I say, "not while you are angry with me."

"Why should you worry if I'm angry with you? You obviously have other women who are not."

"I have no other women. Believe me. You are my only love."

"It is no wonder you refuse to speak to my father about our marriage. You have no intention of marrying me."

"I will speak today. This very day. I love you. There is no other woman — Merytaten — beloved of Sothis."

She stops struggling to pull her arm away and looks at me cautiously.

"You will speak to my father? *This* day?"

"Yes," I say recklessly. Suddenly time seems very, very short and I curse myself for having wasted as much of it as I have.

Her anger disappears like darkness when the Aten appears. She flings her arms around my neck and kisses me breathlessly.

"Now! This very moment!" she cries. "Before you change your mind."

The dog Bel has seen the commotion and decides to join in despite the heat. He rushes round and round us barking and wagging his tail. There are tears of happiness in Merytaten's eyes. I can feel them welling in mine too, but my joy is mixed with fear.

The Sleeping Spell

"My lord," General Horemheb stands very straight before the king, and I can see the veins on his neck and in his hands. He is frustrated and angry, but keeping himself under control. Nefertiti stands behind her husband's chair with her arms around his shoulders, and her chin resting on his head. Her eyes never leave Horemheb. His never leave the king. I can feel their awareness of each other like a tangible but invisible thread between them.

Akhenaten is looking relaxed, enjoying the embrace of his favourite wife. The presence of his friends and family gives him confidence in the company of the man who has always made him uneasy. Tadukhipa, his young Mitannian wife descended from his own grandmother's royal line; Ankhesenpaaten, his daughter-wife; Nezem-mut, not as beautiful as her sister Nefertiti, but nevertheless a good friend, and I — all surround him. Merytaten is not present. She is sad because I have not kept my word and spoken to her father about our marriage.

"My lord, forgive me if I speak my mind. It is the mind of a man of honour, a loyal and trusted servant of your father — "

"I am the king now," Akhenaten says easily. "Are you *my* loyal and trusted servant, General?"

Horemheb's colour deepens. "Of course, my lord . . . I meant only — "

89

"I know what you meant, General. I respect you as my father respected you. You have my permission to speak as freely as you wish."

"I have been honoured to serve both your father and yourself, sir, as Commander-in-Chief of your armies, as judge of your criminals, as ambassador to the vassal states of your empire, as superintendent of your tribute collections. . . ."

"I know your titles, General. Speak to me of your mind. A man's mind is more interesting to me than a hundred thousand titles."

"I meant only that the mind of an ordinary man may be confused and undisciplined, but that the mind of the holder of such titles may not be."

"Speak," Akhenaten says, still unruffled, his right hand going to his left shoulder to take hold of Nefertiti's, turning his head slightly to let his lips rest upon her slender fingers for a moment.

Do I sense the tension in the handsome general increase? I love my friend the king, but he seems more and more insensitive to the undercurrents of feelings around him. He is even taking Nefertiti's love for granted these days, never doubting that she and everyone around him is equally as excited about the abstract beauty of the new philosophy, equally obsessed with the intricate working of the eternal light within the heart.

Horemheb is concerned with the immediate. The great empire built up by Thutmose III and maintained, after a fashion, by Akhenaten's father, is beginning to disintegrate. The Amorites and the Hittites are on the move. Loyal vassals are pleading for assistance to resist them, and not-so-loyal vassals are taking the opportunity to break away. The rich flow of tribute which has been pouring into the Two Lands since the time of Thutmose III, bringing with it general prosperity, and private luxury for the royal household and the priests of Amun, is beginning to dry up.

Horemheb speaks now, long and passionately, on the need for a strong hand to hold the reins of the empire, the need to enforce the tribute laws, the need to send troops to teach the rebels a lesson.

"You hold in your hands the crook and the flail, my King," Horemheb says. "You have used the crook. Now it is time to use the flail."

Akhenaten listens to him patiently, his eyes becoming thoughtful, his chin in his hand, Nefertiti's arms pushed aside.

"And what if I believe that the Aten shines on all men and its light seeks all men's hearts, and only the Aten may join men of different nations together?" he asks quietly.

"The Aten has given the nations into the hand of the pharaoh, my lord, the Aten has put them under the heel of the servant of Aten."

"Oh, really?" says Akhenaten, raising an eyebrow. "I thought you believed it was Amun who had done that."

Horemheb flushes, and I see his knuckles white as he clenches his fists. He bites back what he wants to say.

Akhenaten looks at him amused, relaxed for the moment, and then his face shadows, his eyes narrow.

"My grandfather, and his father before him, were misled by the false god Amun," he says, and now there is a dangerous edge to his voice. I have noticed lately that my king is subject to inexplicable and violent changes of mood, sudden rages that come out of a clear and cloudless sky, the frustration of a far-sighted man looking to the horizon, while his fellow men look no further than the walls that surround their own houses. "Conquering and slaughtering and enslaving is not the way of the Aten. If foreigners are unhappy under our yoke, set them free. We should not have taken their lands in the first place."

"My lord, whether we should or not is another question." I begin to admire Horemheb's self-control. I know he is murderously angry, but his voice barely falters. Akhenaten

91

has asked for plain speaking from his senior officials, and Horemheb goes as close as he dares. "Your grandfathers won for you a great empire, and you owe it to them and to your subjects to hold it firm and strong, that no man may harm a hair of the head of any man in it."

"What is an empire but people who have been conquered and exploited? There were many hairs harmed when we took it."

"A king looks to his own people and takes what they need. This play between nations is expected. The Hyksos conquered us because our kings were weak, and their people needed tribute and land. It was only when Amun put strength in the arm of the great Ahmose that he could drive them from our land and harry them to the far reaches of the world. No one blamed the king for this. All rejoiced. His name will live for ever as the saviour of the Two Lands. It is up to us to use our strength, the strength *he* gave us, to protect the honour and respect he won for us, otherwise the mangy curs of every nation will piss on us."

"I piss on the 'honour' and 'respect' you speak of," Akhenaten says bitterly. "They are the smiling masks over the festering sores of fear and hate — the legacy of Amun. If the nations truly respected and honoured us we would not need to fear that they would pull away from us now."

For a moment I think Horemheb will strike the king. Nefertiti must think so too, because she moves swiftly forward between them.

"My husband is an idealist, General," she says smoothly. "He dreams. He has visions. But though they may seem impractical to you, because you are accustomed only to see with the eyes in your head, I assure you that to one who can see with the long sight of the spirit they are very real and very practical."

Horemheb's eyes smoulder, but he bows stiffly to her and to the king. I know that he does not understand. To him physical presence is all that there is. The *ba* and the *ka*, the spirit that reaches throughout eternity and is aware of its oneness with all that is, and the soul that is the pupa of the spirit, still aware only of itself as individual, are to him empty concepts, for experience has not yet shown him their reality.

Horemheb is kept as an administrator, when he longs to be a general. The despatches from the empire are placed carefully in the records office and the Aten is made entirely responsible for the peace-keeping. I pace through the lovely gardens of the Great Palace and feel uneasy. It is not that I think Horemheb is right, and we should send troops to kill people, but I believe peace-keeping is a positive strategy, perhaps one of the most difficult, complex and important strategies a ruler has to consider. It involves close and careful knowledge of the ways of the people, constant listening to their needs, guidance and help with everything that will be for their good. A happy and contented community, steadily based on a set of enduring and co-operative values, will not easily turn to disaffection. As for invaders — intricate and cunning diplomacy, if timely, can work wonders. Amenhotep Nebma'atre' knew everything that went on in every country that could possibly pose a threat to his empire. His spies were posted everywhere, their despatches read meticulously. Trouble was attended to long before it became trouble. Foreign princes were enticed to the colleges of the Two Lands, foreign princesses married into his harem. A continuous stream of bribes — Nubian gold, Sinai turquoise, fine linen, exquisite furniture — flowed to the Hittite, Amorite, and Mitannian kings and the rulers of the vassal states. Over the long years of his reign Amenhotep had developed the strategy of peace as skilfully as ever Thutmose III had developed the strategy of war.

Akhenaten is interested in neither. He believes that once the country is united under one true and incontrovertible religion, once every man, woman and child has put its faith and its future in the far-reaching hands of the Aten, a great peace will come. With Khurahtaten's teaching in my heart I believe this too — but I am ill at ease with the way he is making the transition. At first we talked about a gradual weaning, a gradual education. But the recalcitrance of the priesthood, unwilling to give up their livelihood and their privileges, and the stubbornness of the people in holding to time-worn superstitions, has made him impatient. And impatience clouds the mind. He is using force to topple the old temples down, stringent laws to forbid the worship of old and comfortable gods. Trusting no one to interpret his vision for him, he has made himself the sole companion of the Aten, the sole interpreter of the God's wishes.

In vain I suggest that though Hathor, Isis, Ptah and the others may not be the supreme God, they represent at least aspects of the supreme being. They have a part to play in the gradual awakening to full spiritual consciousness, just as within a school different teachers work on developing different capacities in a child, some discarded as it develops beyond them, others taking their place to carry the child further. But my friend, my brother, my king tells me that the "teachers" I speak about can no longer be trusted . . . their teaching has lost its potency, their priests teach the ancient myths by rote, and no one looks to the original meanings.

"Dead myths are like stones tied to the legs of a man thrown into water. Cut the thongs that bind them to him, and let him swim freely, seeking the sun's light."

"But the sun's light may be too strong to look at directly," I say quietly. "Are not myths often the only way we can seek it out and gaze on it?"

"Ah, living myths," he says. "*Living* myths, my friend."

I bow. There is a truth in this.

Akhenten hates to leave his new city, but he needs to

supervise the building of the new temples he has ordered throughout the Two Lands. I am the only man he completely trusts, and he asks me to leave Akhetaten and travel to distant places for him. Basking in his love I still cannot bring myself to tell him what Ma-nan and Na-aghta have told me about my parentage: and without revealing that, I cannot ask for Merytaten's hand.

Away from the protective ambience of Akhetaten prospering in the hope of a new age, I find a sense of gradual dissolution. It is as though the boy who normally keeps the bullocks walking their endless circular path has fallen asleep, and the cogged and creaking wheels that draw the life-giving waters for the irrigation ditches are slowing down, the water now the merest trickle. The temples that have been the hub of the cities and the villages are lying for the most part deserted, weeds already cracking the paving-stones, wind-blown sand seeking the inner sanctuaries. City and village life continues, of course, but it seems to me there is a lassitude about getting things done, a feeling that no one would care or notice whether a new building was built, or an old one repaired. Wherever I go, I am followed by people complaining about the way the officials are exploiting them, the way the young are running wild.

"They care for nothing," the middle-aged fathers complain. "When I was young I worked from sun-up to sun-down and was proud of my work, but now they hang about on street corners in gangs, their only interest is chasing girls and beating each other up."

"The streets are not safe any more," mothers complain. "Our daughters are afraid to go out."

How sad, I think. *How sad that such breadth and beauty of vision should be lost like a flash storm in the desert. Ah, my friend, my brother, my King, you go too fast for your fellow man. You destroy the old order before the new has taken root in the heart.*

Everywhere I go, I listen and watch and note. I send letter

after letter to the king, advising him what should be done to carry his vision out into the world beyond the shining walls of Akhetaten, but when he replies, he answers nothing in my letters. He speaks of family matters, or of how he has held a festival for Aten and the entire population of the city has joyfully attended. He speaks of a hymn he is preparing for the tomb of Ay, his father-in-law. In a letter I receive at Lunu he quotes from it (though he warns me the final version will be more polished):

"Beautiful is your appearing in the horizon of heaven, you living sun, the first who lived! You rise in the eastern horizon and fill every land with your beauty. You shine and are high above every land. Your rays, they encompass the lands so far as all that you have created. You are Ra. You are far off, yet your rays are upon earth.

"When you go down in the western horizon, the earth is in darkness as if it were dead. They sleep in the chamber, their heads wrapped up, and no eye perceives the other. Though all their things were taken, while they were under their heads, yet they would not know it. Every lion comes forth from his den, and all worms that bite. Darkness . . . the earth is silent, for he who created it rests in his horizon.

"When it is dawn, and you rise in the horizon and shine as the sun in the day, you dispel the darkness and shed your beams. The Two Lands are in festival, awake, and standing on their feet, for you have raised them up. They wash their bodies, they take their garments, and their hands praise your arising. The whole land, it goes about its work.

"All creatures are content with their pasture, the trees and herbs are verdant. The birds fly out of their nests and their wings praise your *ka*. All wild beasts dance on their feet, all that fly and flutter — they live when you arise for them. . . .

"Ah, beautiful is the rhythm of your setting and your rising. Each day a renewal and re-affirmation."

But I know that the day and the night my king sings about is not only, as it appears to be, the day and the night of the sun I see before me now.

I travel the length and breadth of the Two Lands, from the turquoise mines of the eastern desert, where I order a temple to Aten on the site of the old dream chambers where the miners used to seek inspiration and instructions, to as far west as the great lake She-resy, the home of Sobek the crocodile god, and the ancient labyrinth of Amenemhet-Enkh where all the numerous gods of the Two Lands had their shrines under one vast roof. I visit the busy ports in the northern delta where the trade-ships plying the Great Green bring beautiful slender vases from the Mycenaean islands, Phoenician silver, and timber from Byblos.

In the far south, in Nubia, I travel on pack donkeys deep into the interior, sometimes on rocky tracks so precipitous and narrow I think each moment will be my last. Everywhere I carry the message of the One God, who shines on all. Everywhere I put the king's seal on plans for new buildings to his honour and authorize defacement of the old gods in his name.

In his beautiful city Akhenaten describes on more than one stele the special relationship he has with his God.

"You are in my heart, and there is none other that knows you except your son, Neferkhepruré, Sole-one-of-Ra, whom you make to comprehend your design and might. . . ."

I return to Akhetaten in time for the distribution of honours. The streets are crowded with people trying to glimpse the Son of the Sun and his family. They fall back as

I stride through, many recognizing me as the king's closest companion, and priest of Aten. As I approach the palace and the Window of Appearances, the restless movement of people jostling to get a better position, and the hubbub and chattering die down. The crowds within sight of the Window are silent and orderly, bowing in awe before their divine king. Each charioteer is beside his chariot, a groom holding the horses, while he makes obeisance. The fan-bearers are in neat rows, the bowmen, the servants of the royal household, the officials from distant cities and their retinues.... All are bent almost double, their faces lifted to the rays of light coming from their king, as flowers lift to the sun, their hands with palms towards him raised in respect. I take my place among the priests of the Aten as discreetly as I can, responding to their murmured greetings with a nod and a smile, bowing with the rest. Our position is a good one and I have a clear view of the Window. Akhenaten and Nefertiti are naked apart from their crowns, but their skin has been rubbed with gold dust and they gleam like the sun. I have not seen my king go this far before, but I know it has been in his mind. He wants to make a point — and is making it. From his hands flow gifts: jewels and menat collars, goblets and exquisite jars of precious unguent. Bek, his chief sculptor, is receiving gifts, I see, and the goldsmith Pa-ren-nefer. Merytaten, among her sisters, her gold limbs shimmering in the sunlight, leans forward to hand over a slender alabaster vase to the wife of Bek. My heart stirs to her beauty, and the beauty of her mother, holding her youngest child in her arms.

Akhenaten sees me and indicates that I must approach. Embarrassed that I am still in my travelling clothes, I move forward, bowing with every step. His eyes seem glazed when I am near enough to look into them, but it may be the effect of the decoration he has around them, drawn with kohl, with malachite, with lapis lazuli. . . .

He hands me gifts with his golden hands, and I feel no

connection between us. I cannot believe this is my friend. There is such remoteness. It is as though he is inhabited by his god. Behind his shoulder, I see Merytaten's lovely eyes alight with joy that I have returned.

After the ceremony, when everyone has dispersed, I go into the palace. Merytaten runs to me at once and flings herself in my arms, the gold dust from her body rubbing off on me. I have been away a long time, and in that time she has matured a great deal. It is almost a woman's rounded breast that presses so eagerly against mine. I kiss her as I would kiss a woman, and for a while everything else disappears.

For the moment we are aware only of each other — but the moment has to pass. Akhenaten puts his hand upon my shoulder, and from his expression I see that he does not approve of my obvious passion for his eldest daughter.

When we are alone he speaks of it.

"I love you as a brother," he says gently, "but. . . ."

"I am not fit to marry your daughter," I finish the sentence for him.

"You are fit. Certainly you are fit, if she were not the eldest princess of the royal household. Take one of the younger princesses with my blessing. But Merytaten has to marry my heir."

"I love Merytaten."

"She is beautiful and wise. We all love her. But I have no sons, and she must give undisputed legitimacy to my heir."

There is a long silence between us. I weigh the words I am about to say very carefully.

"What if I were indeed your brother?"

Akhenaten laughs.

"What if Horemheb were pharaoh!"

"The king your father had another son, by a wife more royal than your own mother."

Akhenaten's face clouds suddenly.

"What are you saying?"

"I am the son of your sister Sitamon and your father."

Why does he take the news as such a threat? Does he want his infant brother Tutankhaten to succeed him? Surely I am closer to his heart, the partner to all that he is trying to do?

"You lie!" he says. "My sister has no son."

"She has me."

Akhenaten would like to dismiss my claim as nonsense, but he is beginning to remember his father's strange attitude towards me. He is remembering that Amenhotep called me to his deathbed, and that he was about to say something to me when Nefertiti stepped between us. He is remembering that Tiye turned his father's head away from me and towards himself.

I can see that he is disturbed and needs to think.

I bow.

"I am not claiming the crown, my lord. It is your blessing I want, for the love I bear Merytaten."

"Merytaten belongs to Tutankhaten. He is my heir," Akhenaten says stubbornly. The thoughts I have given him are too new. He has not assimilated them yet.

"You speak a great deal about breaking down the old rigorous rules, my lord. You speak of love being the most important judge of whether an action is right or wrong."

"Love, yes. Love being uniting the heart with the Aten. Not lust of the flesh," he adds harshly. There is something in his tone that makes me realize that he is not just speaking about Merytaten and myself. I have noticed, since my return to Akhetaten, a certain estrangement between Nefertiti and himself. They are still seen arm-in-arm in public, but in private I have felt the tension between them. There have even been bitter jests about their youngest three daughters not being his. I have noticed other things too. The wonderful feeling of hope and excitement, the belief in a new age, is just beginning to lose momentum . . . just beginning to turn sour. There are little satiric carvings of the royal family as monkeys being passed around, and unkind graffiti scrawled on walls. The figure of the pharaoh depicted naked, with all his natural imperfections exaggerated, upsets some of the old school who feel it degrades the idea of the divine King to see him as no different and no better than other humans. Nefertiti's beauty is more to their taste, more in the tradition of the divine pharaonic images they are accustomed to, and on more than one occasion I wonder if they are not turning to Nefertiti more than they are to him, and if he is sensing this and resenting it. She is a shrewd and intelligent woman, and I have never felt completely at ease in her presence. It would not surprise me if she were deliberately cultivating interest in herself at his expense. It would also not surprise me if the rumours were true that her youngest three daughters are not Akhenaten's. Are they Horemheb's? I look at them hard, but can see no proof one way or the other. The image of Nefertiti herself is reflected in their features. Horemheb himself has no children with his own wife.

Ankhesenpaaten is pregnant by her father, and extremely bad-tempered. If a son were born, Tutankhaten would be displaced in the line of succession. Would Merytaten still be needed to seal the matter?

"My love for Merytaten goes deeper than the flesh, my lord," I insist.

Suddenly Akhenaten sighs deeply.

"Sometimes, Sothis, I wish I did not carry the burden of the double crown." He is silent a long time after this, and then he says, but not with as much conviction as before: "Tutankhaten is my heir. It is my mother's wish — and my father's."

"And what if I am your brother?"

"You are the brother of my heart whether you are my father's son or not, but I will hear no more talk of you and Merytaten. I intend to live long, and need an heir much

101

younger than myself. Tutankhaten is the choice of my mother *and* myself."

I am silent. I will wait. Another time he may listen, and give his blessing. I am not the only one to have noticed that his moods are erratic and changeable.

I am surprised he did not make more of my announcement that I am his brother. Perhaps it does not come to him as unexpectedly as I had thought it would.

I bow and take my leave.

Merytaten and I are united now in everything but the king's official blessing. There is a pleasure-palace in the south of Akhetaten at Meru-Aten, where we spend much time walking in the gardens, rowing on the lake, and lying together in her chamber.

"If I bear your child, he will let us marry," she says. I kiss the lids of her eyes and her hair and her breasts and say "Yes", but know that the one will not necessarily follow the other.

My tongue seeks out every secret part of her, and my seed flows in her like the great river itself.

We grow careless, forgetting that just because our love-making is so intensely private to us it can be put to public use. Ma-nan and Na-aghta have not given up, and I receive a message that if I do not arrange to meet them at a certain house in Waset on a certain date, it will be the worse for someone I love. My heart is cold. I tell Merytaten that if I fail to keep the appointment they might bring our secret meetings to the notice of the king.

"What does it matter?" cries Merytaten. "I want them brought to the notice of the king!"

"He has the power to part us."

"No one has the power to part us."

"Ah, my love — if only that were so."

"I'll come with you, and tell them what I think of them."

I had told her a great deal about Ma-nan and Na-aghta,

but not yet the secret of my birth, and what they wanted of me.

"No," I say firmly, "it might be dangerous."

"We will send some of my father's soldiers to arrest them."

I wonder if this is the answer, but fear they will have seen this possibility and made provision. Besides, in some dark and guilty corner of my heart I still harbour the temptation to reach for the crook and the flail. Ma-nan and Na-aghta can give them to me. Or if not them alone, then Horemheb, who appears to be in league with them. My conscious mind has totally rejected their offer and my conscious attitude to my king is totally honourable: but that little maggot still gnaws where no light reaches. I suppose I hope that somehow I will be able to have Merytaten and the throne, and still keep an honourable friendship with Akhenaten. A co regency, perhaps.

Anger at myself and fear of the danger we are in causes me to seize her fiercely, kissing her so hard and deep she struggles to draw back, her eyes suddenly alarmed. I hold her thighs and thrust into her so savagely she cries out. When I am done it is my turn to be ashamed. What kind of loving is that, I ask myself. It is no more than a cry of fear, a desperate attempt to fuse us together so that we may never be parted. But — and I look at her hurt and angry eyes — have I not brought about the opposite of what I wanted? For the first time, I look into her eyes after love-making and know that she has not been with me.

"I'm sorry," I say humbly, my voice breaking huskily.

She looks at me for a moment, puzzled, and then draws me close into her arms again.

"It's all right," she whispers. "You must have had your reasons."

I kiss her very, very tenderly now and touch her where she needs to be touched — but gently. She winces at first, but then sighs, and slowly, slowly I bring her to the point where everything is loosened, everything flows, and sweetness of feeling is beyond words.

I go to Waset.

The mighty priest of Amun, who had lived in luxury like a king, greets me in a house like any other house, a small entrance courtyard, a small, dark, cool room leading off from it; no more than three or four rooms in all beyond that.

He is alone: I, ill at ease. Since I received the message I have discovered in my own experience the reason why oracles are supposed to be celibate. My mind is in turmoil. All the levels of my love for Merytaten are active. I feel her in my body, in my mind, in my soul. I cannot reach to the level where I am spirit. I cry to Khurahtaten for help, but I have lost the skill of going into the silence. I have lost the means of reaching him. I cannot feel anything but anxiety that she will be harmed, that I will have brought harm to the person I love most in life.

Why? I cry bitterly to Nut, as she stretches over me, dark and vibrant with stars; the little boat I am on pushing through the black water, the cool night wind filling its sail. *I am trying so hard to bring about good in the world. Why . . . why . . . why does it always turn into evil?* I know my words are unreasonable. I know the wording of the question is wrong. Only the arid desert, where it is flat as a paved floor, has no shadows, and even there, though it cannot be seen, the darkness bides beneath each grain of sand. Light and dark is the pattern of life. It is so. I cannot change it. Rather should I ask: "Now that this evil has come to me how should I transform it into good?"

My love for Merytaten might be distracting me from using my skills as oracle, but it has given me other advantages, confidence in myself as man for one, and a greater understanding of what it means to be human. I had in the past perhaps been too concerned with reaching directly after spirit, almost ignoring the fact that I am also body and soul. I look at Na-aghta's bitter, triumphant face and know that the twist on it comes from something that has happened to him in his life that he has not been able to accept and transform, and has nothing to do with me.

Na-aghta, friend, I think, *let it go before it destroys you.*

I no longer feel nervous. I know who I am and what I am doing.

"You threatened me, Na-aghta?" I say, giving him no titles.

"You and your king have tried to destroy me," he replies coldly.

"No," I say. "No man can destroy another. It can only be the man's gift to himself."

He scowls.

"Don't preach at me, priest. I know the games you play."

I acknowledge his words with a bow, but my eyes are wary. It is true that if he destroys me it will be only with my own connivance, resigning myself to the dark, abandoning hope — but my love for Merytaten is strong, and shouts from my whole being. If he were to touch her, immortal as she is, I know I would have no strength or courage left, no capacity of transformation, no life worth living. Ah —there is my weakness!

He smiles. He can read my mind easily.

"You can save the princess if you wish," he says smoothly, smiling, knowing what he knows.

I look at him, but say nothing. Waiting.

"The infant Tutankhaten is too young to rule . . . but you are of the right age and of the royal line."

"The Two Lands has a king," I say sharply.

"I am a seer," he says slyly. "I have knowledge that the king will not live long."

"You lie. You are no seer. If you have that knowledge it is because you plan to murder him!"

105

"Watch what you think, my lord. Every thought is an action."

"Watch what *you* think, sir. Your thoughts are treason."

"Who will call me to account?"

"I will."

"You forget the princess."

"I left the princess in good hands. She is with Nezem-mut, her aunt."

Na-aghta smiles mockingly. "Nezem-mut is General Horemheb's future wife."

"*Never,*" I shout, shocked, and now no longer confident. If I had not been so concerned every moment of the day to be with my love I would have noticed a net of intrigue tightening round the court. Looking back now, I see it. Is Akhenaten aware of it? I doubt it. It is I who should have warned him. It is I who should have protected him. At this moment I am bitterly ashamed of my obsession with Merytaten.

"I offer you the princess as wife. I offer you the Kingdom of the Two Lands," Na-aghta says softly.

I can hear my heart beating.

A few years ago it was enough that I walked about in the sunshine and had a name, now do I covet so much more?

He notices my hesitation, and waits.

I hear a faint sound behind me, and turn to find Ma-nan, dark-cloaked, standing in the doorway. I wonder if I will get out of this room alive if I refuse. This would not worry me so much if Merytaten were not under their dark shadow. Perhaps, I think, perhaps if I let them kill me, they will spare her. After all, they will want her blood-line to legitimize the next of their candidates. Something moves on my left. I swing round and face a giant cobra with a golden eye. It is raised to strike but pauses, as though held in thrall by Ma-nan's dark powers. To the right, another sound, and there I sense a form so loathsome that the devourer of hearts so frequently depicted in tombs would

106

seem beautiful in comparison. It is the shadow of slime, the slime of shadow, formless yet moving to take on every disgusting form I can conceive of. For a moment I fancy I glimpse Merytaten's exquisite body being sucked into it, hear her desperate cry for help.

"Enough!" I shout. It requires a tremendous effort of will to convince myself that the images are only illusion. But I succeed, and they vanish instantly. I am alone with the two men, but I have seen enough to know what they can do to Merytaten if they choose, and I know that her resistance to them may be considerably less than my own. Or will the innocence of her heart protect her where the guilt of mine cannot?

"I can't give you my answer now. I need to think about it," I say, believing that in this way I will be able to leave the room and warn my king.

"We'll hold the princess until you have decided," Na-aghta says. "If you warn Akhenaten, she will die."

"And not easily," Ma-nan adds darkly.

I round on him.

"What do you hope to gain from me?" I shout. "I am a priest of Aten and will uphold its worship even when I am king."

"We do not ask that Aten be abandoned," Na-aghta says quietly. "Only that Amun, our father, be reinstated."

Will I do that? Will I? What makes them think this? It is true that my vision is not always the same as the king's: but then, is any person's the same as another's? I have thought more than once that if I were king I would somehow integrate the old religion with the new, rather than try to abolish it altogether. I would make adjustments, change emphasis, bring to the surface the forgotten deeper meanings of the ancient images.

Suddenly I feel deathly cold. I realize it is not because I have a different vision that they want me as pharaoh, but because they have established power over my mind and body. Even now I find I cannot move my limbs. I am slipping back under their control.

"Khurahtaten!" I call. No sound from my lips. Only my mind forming the word of his name, my heart the love I bear him. He is here. I know he is. But he cannot reach me. I have put barriers up against him in my arrogance. Through my desire to stand alone, I now stand alone.

Ma-nan is forcing his ugly images on me, surrounding me with ghouls. I can feel a scream of terror rising in my throat — and then . . . and then it comes to me that if they can do this, *so can I*. A dark and fearful horde of images come racing to my mind, and with a bitter inner violence I project them outwards. I see Na-aghta blanch, and then Ma-nan stagger. A fierce joy possesses me. *I too can play this game.* I too can make people cringe in terror, plead for mercy. The thrill of it makes me forget all else. The sense of power, of revenge, is intoxicating. I want to go on and on. I want to kill them with this new and deadly weapon I have discovered in myself. And indeed I might have done so, had they been defenceless ordinary people . . . but after the first shock they rally and for a long, tense moment we stand at stalemate — in empty darkness — impotent and powerless to hurt each other.

It is I who crack first. I can feel my concentration slipping. I can feel the return of fear. I fling myself at the door before it gets out of control. I use all my strength, and burst out into the close, hot streets of the city. I shoulder people aside as I run. I think of nothing but of getting away.

It is only when I am on the boat returning to Akhetaten that the full significance of what I have done dawns on me. Ma-nan has won. I have become no better than he. I can always in the end run away from Ma-nan — but will I ever escape the dark stain that is now on my own heart?

The boat cuts through the waters of the great river. I weep: filled with shame.

On my return to Akhetaten I find that Merytaten has been taken ill. The physician cannot decide what is the matter with her, and Nefertiti and the king are by her side, deadly afraid that she will be taken from them as little Maketaten was. When I hear the news I am in despair. This is Ma-nan's work, surely. With a chill heart, I hurry to her side. I have no confidence that I will be able to help her, now that I have taken the darkness into my own soul.

She is lying very still, very pale.

"She has no fever," the physician tells me. "It is almost as though she has ceased to live, and yet cannot die."

I lean over her, calling her name, thinking without hope that perhaps her illness could have been caused by her fears for me, and now that I am safe returned she will instantly recover. It is indeed a false hope. She does not move. Even her eyelids are still — no dreams disturbing the no man's land where she has gone.

"It is enchantment," Nefertiti says anxiously. "There is no other explanation possible."

My eyes give me away.

"What do you know of it?" she demands.

I cannot answer her. How can I tell them what has passed between those demon priests and myself, and what will save their daughter's life? I am aware that the room has gone very quiet, and everyone is staring at me. Akhenaten's eyes are full of such pleading misery, it almost breaks my heart to see them; the high colour of anger is beginning to stain Nefertiti's cheeks.

"What have you done to her?" she cries.

"Nothing. I have done nothing. I swear it!" How easily the lie is spoken. I am blind, deaf, dumb on all the rich and varied levels of my being. I have forfeited my inner strength; the help of Khurahtaten; the help of my god.

Seeing that she suspects me of causing Merytaten's illness, and seeing the emotions in my face, Akhenaten begins to suspect me too, and in his suffering seizes my

109

arms and shakes me, thrusting his face close to mine.

"I told you you could not have her. Is this your work? Is it?"

He is not as strong as I, but his passion makes him strong, and my guilt weakens me. What have I done to this beloved friend who asked me to leave his daughter alone? It is because I love her she is lying here. It is because I love her that she will die.

"I love her," I cry out at last, and the suffering in my voice will surely convince them that I am innocent. "I could not harm her. I would not harm her. If anyone's it is the work of — " I pause. Behind the queen I have just noticed her sister, Nezem-mut.

Nezem-mut may be as plain as her sister is beautiful, but I have always liked her. Surely, surely it cannot be possible that she would — but Na-aghta has said that she is to be the wife of Horemheb. If I could do what I have done, who knows what dark passions surge in Nezem-mut's apparently calm breast? I find it significant that as soon as I look at her she turns her back, and goes to stare out of the window. I can feel her agitation without even seeing her eyes. Is she caught in the same spider's web as I?

"Nezem-mut," I say in a low voice, so low that no one hears, not even Akhenaten who is almost on top of me. But Nezem-mut hears. She turns, her face red and swollen with tears.

"This is the work of the priests of Amun," she bursts out, almost choking on her sobs. The eyes of everyone in the room are drawn to her now, and I am as instantly forgotten as the loser in a race. I see her caught in the charged beams of their attention, and pity her distress. She is torn, racked, tortured. She loves Merytaten, I know. Who would not? But Na-aghta and Ma-nan, possibly even Horemheb, must have used her in some way, as they have used me in the past and are using me now.

"Why do you say that?" asks Nefertiti, her eyes blazing

110

like black fire. Her sister flings herself at her feet, beating her head on the ground. I rush forward without thinking and put my arms around her, lifting her up. I don't know what I intend to do. Perhaps I am afraid that if she confesses I, too, will be implicated. I don't know what I think. The power of the dark priests is in the room. Of that one thing I am sure.

Akhenaten suddenly loses control completely. In his mind at this moment there is no doubt that Nezem-mut is right — his daughter's illness is due to the malevolence of the priests of Amun. The hate he bears them knows no bounds. He forgets everything — the vision of his god of light, his belief in peace and love and understanding. . . . He turns and rushes to the door shouting for the vizier and the captain of his guards.

"Arrest every priest of Amun you can find, and if they resist, kill them!"

He has tried to obliterate the dark side of magic by teaching that God is light: tried to break the occult stranglehold of the priests by stressing that the one and only god's healing, protecting, helping rays shine down upon the royal family, and through them are transformed and dispersed throughout the world: tried to control just this kind of corrupt and dangerous use of natural forces. He knows now he has failed; and in his failure he has probably lost his second daughter.

Inside the room, it is as though time has been frozen. The physician is poised beside a brazier where he has been burning herbs, Nefertiti and I are close to Nezem-mut, who has her hands to her face, even her tears apparently arrested in this long and brittle moment. On the couch with its golden lion paws and golden lion head behind the ivory and ebony head-rest, Merytaten lies, exquisite, pale, totally motionless, fine linen covering her from foot to breast. It seems to me I see the wings of a bird folded around her, shimmering with light as though the sun is

111

reflected off rippling water. I remember my own experiences in the House of Many Thresholds, and wonder if her ka is hovering in the room, listening to us, watching us . . . trying to speak. . . . I curse myself for allowing myself to become so embedded in fear and darkness that I cannot reach her.

Break free! I cry deep in my heart. *There is a way. You are a child of Light. Call on the Beings of Light to help you!*

And then it seems to me the shimmering light around her intensifies — but even as I begin to hope, a sound breaks the silence of the room, and I spin round in time to see Nefertiti strike her sister a second time across the face. The atmosphere in which Merytaten might have achieved her freedom is shattered. I seize her mother's wrist angrily, and hold her back from a third blow.

"You both know something," she spits out. "I can feel it. Tell me!"

I find that I am holding her arm, and the arm of her sister. It is as though we form a triangle, and I can feel the force of Nefertiti's will driving through us, taking us over. She, too? I am alarmed. As her husband's partner in both religious and state matters she has achieved much that is on the side of light, and I doubt if Akhenaten could have achieved as much alone. But she has always had a restless energy that could just as easily be harnessed for evil as for good. I, at least, am aware of what I have done and will guard against it in the future — but she is not so quick to analyse her motives and her feelings, and may go too far.

With an effort I break the contact.

"We know nothing," I say wearily. "We suspect it is the work of Na-aghta of Amun."

"Why? Why do you suspect *him* of all the Amun priests we have displaced?"

"He is a man of great force, and great determination."

"And what else?"

"Personal hatred of the king."

"And what else?"

She is no fool. Her eyes bore into mine. Nezem-mut has taken advantage of the respite from questioning to kneel beside her niece's bed, holding the pale hands and sobbing, praying to all the gods of the Two Lands for help in restoring her.

"You hear?" snaps Nefertiti. "My own sister, and she calls on demons at a time like this!"

"Not demons, my lady, she calls on them only as aspects of the One God — the many hands of Aten. . . ."

"So! You would change my husband's teaching!"

"No, my lady. Draw out of it what is already there."

"He has forbidden the names of the old gods to be invoked. He has forbidden their mention in this city, in this land."

"As gods, yes, but surely as aspects of — "

She strides to the door and calls the guards.

Within seconds Nezem-mut and I are marched away as prisoners. Stunned and horrified, I look over my shoulder to see the outer shell of my love still lying unmoving on the bed, the lovely, flickering winged light gone, only darkness surrounding her.

The Release

Darkness should not worry me, but it does. There is no measure of time here, where Ra is not seen to rise or set. I cannot see the stars. The moon has become a myth of pearl, pregnant with secrets. How brief my freedom was, how sweet and fragile. Did I dream Merytaten? Did I dream her limbs intertwined with mine, the trust in her eyes, the sudden laughter and the sharing of thoughts? In this bare hole I ponder on many things, not least that my king of light, my dreamer, poet, mighty channel of God's will on earth, keeps such prisons in his beautiful city and has no pity for those who must endure them. Are his eyes now so blind with light that he does not see the darkness under each grain of sand, let alone in his own heart? God is Light, yes, but also Maat and Thoth and Ptah; Osiris, Isis, Horus; Hathor and even Set. Justice and Order, Wisdom and Truth, Creator of Form, Giver of Life, Resurrector of the Dead, Challenger and Destroyer. We may have gone wrong in worshipping each aspect of God as though it were a separate being, forgetting the whole when we worship the part, but is he not committing the same error, choosing light as the sole attribute and dismissing all the others as subsidiary? Who are we to divide the One into the Many, but who is he to choose one of the many and give it the status of the One? His

114

revolution will fail because it is not grounded on the whole truth, but only on a part of it. In my darkness I see the shape of his defeat and weep. But need I weep? Whatever happens he has made men question what had become dead ritual, and no matter how those who overthrow him try to erase his name from the record, he will live for ever, and whenever the flow of communication between god and man becomes choked with weeds and debris, men will stir to his voice again, and try to unblock the channel, free the flow.

And I, will I be remembered? Will I remember? This darkness gives me a taste of death, without the resurrection. Strange how different this cell of stone feels to the House of Many Thresholds. There is no going out or coming in here, only abiding despair. The weight of others who have suffered here oppresses me, holds me to the place. I waste precious time in misery and bitterness, until a fine, small voice at last makes itself heard.

> *Passing in and out of my body*
> *my soul sees*
> *what I do not see,*
> *hears what I do not hear.*
> *When he sings*
> *the birds listen.*
> *When he weeps*
> *the Great Ocean*
> *absorbs his tears.*
> *When he teaches me*
> *I learn.*
> *When I am tired*
> *he lifts me.*
> *What perversity*
> *makes me*
> *want to stand alone,*
> *a dry stick*

115

> *in a field of corn,*
> *a dry stick*
> *cracking in the wind?*

What perversity indeed? I turn around from wasteful darkness and reach for my strength. My king, my brother, my friend is in danger. I can feel it. That he should leave me here is proof that he is allowing himself to be manipulated by dark forces. Whether they are outside himself or within makes no matter. I compose myself, and work on my old techniques for reaching out beyond the limits of my physical body to that world which is in neither time nor space.

If I had not allowed myself to be tumbled on the beach by every emotional breaker, I would have been able to swim out to the deep ocean much earlier and draw from it the wisdom I need. Now at last I have the strength to do it. My counsellor; my guide, Horus-Khurahtaten, is here in answer to my call. Together we will see what can be done.

Soul-flight is easy when the heart is right and the world is stripped away. My dark prison cell becomes a sycamore branch, on which my soul-bird pauses before taking off. The falcon and I soar, the yellow dust of Set's desert flowing from our wings like smoke, Osirian green glancing off our feathers like sunlight.

At first the freedom intoxicates me. What could I not do as soul, untrammelled by the body? But the eye of Horus is on me and I know the task I have been set is all that I will have time for now . . . is all that I am ready for.

Things are at first confusing. How many would-be soul-travellers report back untruths, for no other reason than that they are unused to seeing with the eyes of the soul, and even more unused to describing what they see in the limited and limiting vocabulary of the physical world when they return?

116

Deep in my heart lie the images of the great spirits that my people call the gods. Generations of belief have put them there, and I find my thoughts fly to them now as the easiest way to understand what I am seeing.

It is at first as though I am floating through the world as I know it; unseen, but seeing. And then it is as though I see the same space my world is occupying inhabited by innumerable other beings, usually invisible to me, flowing through each other like the cross-currents in a river, apparently not aware of each other, yet affecting each other none the less.

Then I am in regions for which I can find no analogy.

Is it Thoth's voice I hear deeply vibrating in my heart, my earth-ears catching no whisper of the words, yet my earth-tongue already struggling to give shape to the sounds that are not sounds?

"I am Thoth, he who is the writing reed of the inviolate god, the lord of laws, whose words are written and whose words have dominion over the two worlds. . . . I am Thoth, who prepares tomorrow and who foresees what will come afterwards. I have dispelled darkness, and driven away the storm. . . ."

The chant, that is not a chant, is taken up by another. Hathor — whose breath is the scent of the sycamore in flower, whose blood is the green sap of the world, whose breast-milk sustains us as our limbs grow, whose music brings joy to our hearts. . . .

Then Isis, whose fierce love protects us; who mends the broken, nurses the sick; whose mother-heart will never let us perish no matter how we are beset by enemies; Lady of the marshes, who solved the secret of the tamarisk tree and brought her husband back to life. . . . Even Apep, the dark serpent, the destroyer, trembles at her name. . . .

I have hardly time to adjust to the strangeness of the realms we are passing through when Khurahtaten calls to me, his voice a falcon cry. Now we are above the desert cliffs to the east of Akhetaten. Below us the dry dust swirls and eddies where workmen have made paths to the tomb of my pharaoh; the mountains crouch; the gullies, where storms have washed away the sand, lie serpent-like far below. The shadows are sharp and black in contrast to the blazing light of the sun.

Why are we here? I wonder. *I want to speak with my brother the king in his palace.* A sudden chill thought strikes me. Is he dead? Is he dead already?

"No," says Horus-Khurahtaten quietly. "There is still time."

We plunge like the birds we are, and steeply the rock-faces hurtle by, rock on rock, layered through time like man's reaching and failing. In a dark gash of shadow a deeper shadow crouches — the entrance to the tomb Akhenaten is having built for himself and his family. The sad little daughter Maketaten is already lying there.

If he is not dead, I think, *why are we here?* But there is no time for further questioning: we are inside the tomb, our wings folded, passing like smoke through the mighty corridors. The entrance, a dark slit in the rock of a mountain had seemed, like man, nothing very much, but inside, again like man, chambers and corridors filled with powerful and symbolic meanings, reaching deeper and deeper into the bedrock. At the time of my going to prison the tomb had not been finished, and I can see that it is still unfinished. Strangely, it is deserted; the usual clamour of hammers, and men moving about and shouting to each other, absent.

Rock-silent the huge central corridor takes us to the chamber where the king will lie in death. On the plaster walls the reliefs are half-finished; some painted, some not; the artist's and the workmen's tools still lying around where they have been put down. The flickering of light that illuminates these details is unexpected. The main chamber is not deserted, as the corridor was.

Within it, at the centre, Akhenaten is lying on a

118

workman's wooden bench: standing behind his head, Nefertiti.

Startled, I look closer, and am relieved to see the shallow rise and fall of his chest. On his forehead, where the uraeus usually rests, lies a large, translucent amethyst crystal. The flickering flames of the tapers and torches in the chamber shining through the crystal cause ripples of purple light to play upon his eyelids.

My spirit companion and myself pause at the doorway, and make no sound. The two in the chamber do not notice us.

I feel uncomfortable. I am witnessing a very private rite, and am torn between thinking that I should leave at once, and anxiety for my friend and king. I myself, through Khurahtaten, have learned a great deal of esoteric crystal-lore, but even I would not lightly dare to do what Akhenaten is now doing. Nefertiti is holding a second crystal above her own head, and the light of the wall-torch shines through it. I notice he has his right hand on his breast, where a scarab carved from amethyst rests. She plays the beam of light that shines through her crystal alternately on the amethysts that lie on his forehead and on his heart, as though she is trying to stimulate some active response from these centres. I know what they are trying to do. Of all the seven colours of light, the purple ray gives the vibrations closest to pure spirit. I suspect that these three amethyst crystals were once of identical size and joined together. Such a trinity is not easy to find — but once found, very powerful, echoing the mighty *Three In One* of the universe: the Creator, the Creation and the active force of the divine spirit that infuses everything and keeps it going.

Nefertiti speaks the secret words from the old texts with confidence, as though they are not new to her. I see by Akhenaten's expression that he is deep in trance.

I fear for them, knowing that there are laws pertaining

119

to this work, and that to break any one of them is to lay oneself open to great danger. One of the most important is purity of motive, and I sense that this one, at least, is being broken. Nefertiti and Akhenaten are trying to free their daughter from the horrifying spell she is under, and that in itself might justify the method they are using had that been their only motive. But they are also seeking to find a revenge spell that will destroy Na-aghta and Ma-nan.

"*Stop!*" I cry — but of course my voice cannot be heard.

Is it possible that, for a second, Nefertiti hesitates? But if she does, it is only for a second.

I recall the time I too used the three amethyst crystals, the Horus violet ray, to reach the knowledge beyond knowledge . . . the voice of my teacher murmuring in my ears.

"Is your motive pure? To help and not to harm?

"Is the will concentrated? You are the potter's hands: if you tremble, the pot is ruined.

"Is your thought clear, do you know what you are doing, and why you are doing it?

"Are you working with love? Remember if there is a grain of hate anywhere in your heart it will deflect the shaft of Light and bring about evil, and not good."

Nefertiti's voice is full of hate.

I try to bring my own will to bear on my friend and king, to counteract hers.

"My lord, be aware . . . be aware of what you are doing. The energy you seek can illumine men's hearts. In that seeing, they can change. Use this energy, not for revenge but to illumine the hearts of the priests of Amun that they see — and, in seeing, change their ways."

Akhenaten stirs, and his eyelids flicker.

Nefertiti looks at him sharply. She is still not aware of our presence at the doorway, but feels something is wrong.

I call out again, and she looks swiftly round the room, her eyes flashing from beneath winged eyebrows like brilliant lightning through storm cloud. Ah, but she is beautiful! The strength of my will falters. Have I misjudged her? What the priests of Amun have done to Merytaten deserves to be punished! I myself long for vengeance. Do I not want to hurt them as they have hurt me? I remember the burning skewers in my feet as a child. I remember the beatings, so carefully delivered that no marks showed, when I was being displayed in the temple. And now the subtler tortures of the mind. . . .

I feel the whiplash of Khurahtaten's anger on my cheek and stop my thoughts in time. He indicates that we must leave and I know that if I cannot help my friend I had better go. To join my hate to his would be disastrous.

I am already back in prison and I am alone. Bitterly, I think how easy it is to hate one's enemies, how difficult to love.

Gradually, in the darkness, wisdom returns and I take hold of the two truths that had nearly slipped from my grasp. One: that there is nothing, no one, that cannot change, transform. The second is that that which is man beyond his nine modes of being — beyond the three groups of three: body, soul and spirit; heart, intelligence and power; shadow, double and name — that which belongs to man even beyond the Duat, to the first thought, has all the energy it needs for moving mountains, transforming hearts. The magic tricks we use, the three amethysts, the green Osirian heart-scarab with its gold thread holding it to the chest of a dead man, the amulets, the elaborate word-spells vibrating the etheric: all these are no more than the counting beads a child uses before it has a clear mental image of numbers.

Akhenaten knows this. This is why he has been trying to stop the trade in amulets, trying to forbid the use of spells, trying to educate the people to reach for a direct relationship with God. He sees himself as the last trick they will need before they are ready. He has spoken to me many times of the moment when he will step back and let the people "touch the rays", as he calls it, themselves.

Ah, Akhenaten, brother, King, why do you seek revenge through spells, like any back-street sorcerer and fallen priest? You have such greatness in you. Magic may be used for good . . . perhaps; but magic used for revenge is hardly worthy of a god-king touched by the rays of the Aten.

How many days after this I stay in prison, I cannot tell. Some days I feel ill and despairing, and am indistinguishable from any other prisoner. On other days I feel strong, and thoughts come to me worthy of my training as oracle and priest. I try to use the time for learning, and in the darkness pretend I am dead, and entering with the sun into the twelve divisions of the Night. With the sun, awakening to life each mansion of the Duat that we enter, bringing joy. . . . I smile to think that as a child I had taken the twelve mansions literally as the hours of the night. Now I see this mighty myth, inscribed on the tombs of kings, in all its rich profundity . . . the huge wheel of Time in which the sun itself is born, lives and dies, is born, lives and dies: the body lying for ever with earth eyes watching the pageant, knowing that everything is renewed, is renewable, while the soul flies in and out of the tomb . . . in and out of the pageant . . . free.

Suddenly, the door of my cell clangs open, and sunlight shatters like glass in my eyes. I bury my head in my arms, the light causing me pain.

I know someone is standing in the doorway, and I know it is my king, but I cannot yet bring myself to stand up and face him.

He waits for me to adjust. Slowly, slowly I lift my head, and blink at him. He is a black shape against a blaze of light. My eyes hurt, and I close them again. He comes forward and takes my hands, helps me to my feet.

"My brother," he says gently, "forgive me."

Now I struggle to open my eyes. *Brother?* He has accepted me as his brother?

He puts his arms round me and holds me close. I can feel the tears on his cheeks.

"There is nothing to forgive," I say quietly; and mean it. I have known anger. I have made mistakes.

"Merytaten . . .?" I breathe her name, but dare not put the question into words.

"The same," he says sadly. "But I have come out of my madness, and I know what we must do."

I remember the ritual of the three amethysts, and fear his meaning. But my eyes are open now, and I can look into his. He is right: the madness of fear and anger is gone. He is calm.

He takes me out of the prison, his arm around my shoulders. My gaolers fall back, and press their foreheads to the ground as he passes. I am returned to the palace and given fine foods to eat, clear wines from the delta vineyards to drink. I can eat and drink very little. I want to sleep.

I sleep.

When I wake a harpist is beside me, playing, and a singer from my temple, with lotus flower on head and in hand, is singing. On a chair by the window my brother is sitting, gazing thoughtfully out at the garden. How beautiful this room is, I think, noting the flowering papyrus tiles on the walls, the ceramic fishes on the floor, the gold and ivory and ebony of the delicately made furniture, but most of all, the sunlight. Everywhere, the sunlight.

The king turns at once when I wake, even before I speak, and comes to embrace me. Then he dismisses the harpist and the singer and sits beside my bed. I lie back, enjoying the luxury of the soft bed thongs after the hard floor of the prison.

"When you were in prison," he says, and he speaks calmly, as though he knows that what has been done

123

cannot be undone — but that I have forgiven him. "When you were in prison I nearly betrayed everything you and I have worked for."

I say nothing, but am relieved. Perhaps my warning thought had reached him after all.

"I tried. . . ." His voice falters.

"I know," I say gently, sitting up and swinging my legs round so that my feet rest on the floor. We look deeply into each other's eyes. Tears begin to gather in his.

"Don't," I whisper, putting my hands on his shoulders. "Brother, don't. . . ."

"I nearly —"

"I know. But you did not. In the end, you did not." I kiss him, as brother kisses brother; not as subject, king. It could not have been easy to turn the power he had against himself and not his enemy, forcing his own transformation from resentment to forgiveness. "Now that we are together," I say, "and we are no longer crippled by hate and fear, we will surely be able to save Merytaten."

"I know it," he says simply.

I wonder about Nefertiti. Has she accepted the change in him? As though in answer to my thought, he tells me that Nefertiti and he have had a disagreement, and that she has retired for a time to the northern palace. Suffering shows in his face, and I know that he loves her still. As king he has had to take other wives, but Nefertiti has always been and will always be his only real love. It was the same with his father (our father) and his wife Tiye. This love overruled everything — even justice. I know this, for have I not been its victim?

I dress, and we walk in the garden, his arm around my shoulders, talking as we used to talk, no barriers, no shadows. We know we will go to Merytaten, but first there are matters to settle between us.

My heart stops beating as he tells me I will be proclaimed his co-regent and his heir. At this moment I think no further than that this will mean I can marry Merytaten. The nest of hornets I will inherit with the honour does not enter my mind. But as he talks I gradually begin to get a picture of what has been happening since I was "put away", and a small, unworthy thought creeps into my mind — that Akhenaten has found the priests of Amun too strong for him, and as he sinks deeper and deeper into trouble, he needs me to help him out. It is not so much that he has had a change of heart, but that he is in a corner, and does not know who to trust any more. He is buying my trust-worthiness by offering me the treasure I want most in the world, his daughter.

I crush the thought angrily, but it leaves a stain.

It seems the capricious arrest of myself and Nefertiti's sister has brought to the surface a great deal of resentment that had been festering unnoticed before. Also the manifest power of the priests of Amun in striking down one of the sun-god's own children (and for the second time) in her own home, many leagues from Waset, had caused dismay and awe. All the things Akhenaten had neglected, all the enemies he had made by trying to push aside the traditional in favour of his own private vision, had added fuel to the fire that was beginning to crackle in the Two Lands. He needed help desperately, and he could trust no one. The head of his army, Horemheb, had been seen visiting the outlawed priests of Amun, and showed a sullen resentment when given any orders by the king. Nefertiti herself seemed to have retreated further and further into a private world where she practised rituals and studied spell charts that were forbidden. He was surrounded by courtiers who flattered, but whom he knew kept lines of communication open secretly to the enemy. Some of the artists who had worked for him were loyal, and Ay, his uncle the master of the chariots, and his father's close friend, remained at his side, though on the strength of this friendship with his father, gave him many a straight talk on how his policies were bringing about the ruin of the Two Lands.

Akhenaten pointed out that his father himself had noticed that the priesthood of Amun were becoming too powerful, and had tried to curb their power and strengthen that of the priests of the Aten.

"But he used diplomacy, not force," Ay said.

"I am not using force," Akhenaten said.

Did he really believe that depriving people of their livelihood, destroying their beliefs, arresting them if they demurred, smashing down their most sacred places, was not force?

I sigh. Change through diplomacy and education takes so long! But it lasts. Yes, it lasts!

We go to Merytaten.

We sit on either side of her, one hand holding hers, the other holding each other's, so that we three are linked. Quietly, we prepare to relax. I cannot dismiss from my mind the uncharitable thought I had had, about Akhenaten's motives in accepting me as brother and co-regent, but I can transform it. I put beside it in my mind the conviction that he indeed has changed, he indeed did refuse to use the amethyst ray for revenge, and chose rather to forgive. The two thoughts lie together, giving me the picture of a man like any other man; a mixture of good and bad, but struggling to make the good in himself win over the bad. We on earth can do no more.

What thoughts he is unravelling, what feelings he is trying to sublimate, I can only guess at, but I know I dare not think of Na-aghta or Ma-nan, and he dare not think of Nefertiti.

We must think only of our love for Merytaten, and our love for each other. The three of us must be linked by love. We must visualize our love like a flow of light coursing through our veins and through each other.

126

Our vision gradually grows stronger until it is as though our love is a sudden flood that washes away evil thought-spells like storm waters wash away the dust from the desert gullies. We think of the great source from whom we have all come, using our ancient symbols as they were meant to be used — not as gods or as men, but as aspects of the one driving force . . . the one will-thought before which there was no other.

We can feel her hands growing warmer. We can see colour coming to her pale cheeks.

We could have done this before, I think sadly, *if only we had not been so full of fear and hate.*

It seems to me that the three of us are floating. The room seems to have dissolved. Now I can hardly feel her hand in mine; but I can hear the beating of her heart in my heart. It is almost as though bubbles of light are floating up around us, and everywhere the light is becoming stronger and stronger. I know we have broken the spell. I know that we are all free.

How long we would have drifted like that in pure bliss I do not know. The opening of the chamber door brings us back to earth.

It is Nezem-mut, pale and thin from her prison experience, but her face is full of relief to see Merytaten sitting up in bed, holding our hands, the three of us laughing like children.

The First Duel

The next months are hectic. We are preparing for our wedding and for my formal installation as co-regent. I am too busy to notice that Na-aghta and Ma-nan have achieved what they wanted to achieve: someone they think they can control on the throne of the Two Lands. Perhaps I no longer see myself threatened by them — Merytaten's love gives me strength, and the infectious confidence of her father lulls me into thinking that all is well. Perhaps I even think the danger to Akhenaten's life has been averted by my joining him on the throne. Although I have changed nothing yet, I intend to try a compromise between the total dedication of Akhenaten to the one aspect of God, light symbolized by the sun's disk, and the traditional myths in which the awesomeness of the concept of God is broken up, as light in a prism. I believe that each image carries some of the truth, but for the whole to be understood it is essential that each must be understood in two ways: in its own individual right *and* in its relationship to the whole. Now I begin to understand the real importance of names. I see the significance of the belief that when the soul goes before the gates in the World-Beyond-Death, it may not pass a single one until it has correctly pronounced the name of the guardian god of that gate. It is not just a matter of naming names, but the cumulative understanding, built up name by name, of the different aspects of God. It is only when all the aspects are individually and collectively grasped that the soul is ready to enter the place of final transformation.

My brother-king chooses for me the name Smenkhkare, which means: "Establishing the spirit of the source of light", and gives me one of Nefertiti's titles, which means: "Beloved of the living Aten".

I am made co-regent, but he tells no one of my relationship to his sister Sitamon, for that would reflect badly on his own mother, who deprived me of my place in my father's house and broke his wife/daughter's heart. The great Queen Tiye had died while I was in prison, and her memory is precious to her son and to her people. I respect this, remembering all that she did that was good. I wonder privately, however, if Akhenaten would have dared to make me co-regent while she was still alive.

Tutankhaten is too young to realize the implications of his displacement, or even that he has been displaced, but it will not be long before others make him aware of it.

Merytaten and I treat every moment we have together as though it might be our last. When we are alone we fall upon each other and make love until we are exhausted; then we rest and make love again.

Ankhesenpaaten's child by her father is born dead, and after a time of bitter mourning she is relieved to find herself without the responsibilities of motherhood. Her father is now too busy and too harassed to think of fathering another child on her, and she lives with her mother and her younger sisters in the northern palace. Each time we see her she seems to have grown older and more worldly-wise.

There is no doubt that intrigue is rife in the northern palace, and although Merytaten longs to be with her mother, each time we visit, she swears it will be the last.

The queen wants Tutankhaten to succeed her husband, as originally planned by Queen Tiye, and in subtle ways makes me feel an intruder. She has been told that I am Sitamon's son, but chooses not to believe it. I see no evidence that Horemheb visits her, nor indeed that her sister Nezem-mut receives any communication from him. I believe Nefertiti genuinely cares for Akhenaten, though she is becoming increasingly impatient with him.

She studies day and night to master the ancient magic. She knows Akhenaten is in danger, and believes she will be able to protect him by countering spell with spell. She looks on me as an opportunist who had the intention of coming to the throne from the very first. I, in my turn, am not sure that she herself does not intend to succeed her husband. I remember the early days sadly. How promising and beautiful everything had seemed then. What dreams we had had of our great city of the sun being a centre of light for the whole world.

One day I tell her that she will destroy her husband, rather than protect him, with the forbidden knowledge she is seeking. She tells me to leave her home and not return.

Miserably, Merytaten walks away with me. She is so young — torn between people she loves; surrounded by shadows, by whispers, by secret messengers coming and going, by old friends who talk smoothly, but whom she can no longer trust. We both sense, when we are not in the forgetful paradise of love-making, that a gigantic shadow is bearing down on us, but we, as though in a nightmare, cannot move our limbs out of its way.

Each day, I tell myself that the next day I will speak to Akhenaten, and we will plan to turn about the process that is causing such disaffection in the country. He is behaving strangely. He spends most of his time in the temple praying to his god and when he comes out and everyone clamours for his attention, for his decision and his commands, he brushes them aside with a gentle smile and a wave of his thin and sensitive hand.

"All is in the hands of the Aten," he says quietly. "Our enemies will not prevail."

I am torn between the naïvety of this, and admiration at the strength of his faith. What if he is right?

I tell Merytaten that he is wrong to think he can overthrow the customs and beliefs of millennia in one lifetime, and that his changes will come about more quickly if, paradoxically, they start more gradually. She resents my criticism of her father.

"What do you know?" she says sharply. "You, too, may only be moving small pebbles about in the dust while the whole world is in danger!"

Her words shock me, and for a moment I lose faith that he or I, or indeed anyone, can ever effect changes in the world of any significance. Then, I remember that even moving one pebble effects a change in its immediate environment, and any change, however small, has a domino effect. Who knows but by moving one pebble one may move a mountain.

One day, the thing I dread, and against which I have been preparing myself, takes place. I, as co-regent, am sent to Waset to take up residence in the old palace, and to sit in judgment on someone caught attempting the assassination of the king. Merytaten will not be parted from me, and insists not only on accompanying me south but on sitting beside me in the throne-room. She looks fragile and small in the great chair her grandmother Tiye used to occupy, and I myself feel inadequate in the seat of the old king. It has been a long time since it was occupied, Akhenaten hating to leave Akhetaten.

The accusers bring the accused forward.

I stare into the cold, dark eyes of Ma-nan.

As far as the laws of the land are concerned, the

131

procedure is clear. The man must be sentenced to death and his name be erased from all records, his body buried without ceremony, and without any mark upon it as to who it once was. He must be returned, in other words, to the great void.

I stare at Ma-nan, remembering my childhood, and how I had feared to enter death without a name, how I had feared extinction . . . until despair had driven me to court it to escape his cruelty. The opportunity for revenge has been given me without my seeking it. Would I be so wrong to take it? Indeed, would it not be an act of treason against my brother-king to hesitate, or to set aside a single item in the expected punishment?

Time remains poised in the judgment hall. In that silence I know that Maat's scales are not in some faraway chamber under the earth where the sun goes at night. They are here, now, always at this moment, and the heart of the living *and* the dead is balanced at every moment against the feather of truth.

Ma-nan's heart is heavy with evil. He knows it, and I know it. He looks at me malevolently, smiling, knowing that I am as much on trial at this moment as he is, waiting for me to fail the test. Merytaten sits upright in her gilded chair, her face painted as a queen's should be, the wings of the vulture crown folded around her ears. On her breast I can see the love-necklace I had given her, one large amethyst flanked by two water-clear quartz crystals and linked by golden ankhs. She has insisted on wearing this, instead of the heavy formal one suitable for such a formal occasion. I can see it rising and falling on her breast more swiftly than it should. On her slender finger she twists our ring, lotus of lapis lazuli held by rods of gold and turquoise. She knows the power of Ma-nan, as I do, and fears him. It is important that I do not give way to fear. Flanked by armed soldiers, clad in shabby clothes very unlike his former robes, he seems a very different adversary now to when he

132

used to terrorize me as a nameless boy. I know that when he was arrested he would have been searched, and there could be no resin to give off hateful smoke, hidden about his body. Nor has he had time to work his word-spells on me. I am in the king's chair, knowing that I am descended from a line of kings, named and powerful.

"This man," I say, slowly and clearly, "shall not be put to death."

A gasp goes round the hall followed by an angry murmur. I dare not look at Merytaten.

I wait for silence, and struggle to suppress thoughts of revenge, knowing that to give way to them will mean that I will forfeit the help of the great eternal spirits when I need them most, and that Horus-Khurahtaten will turn his golden eye from me. I want to cry out for help, but know that this decision has to be made on my own. When it has been made — then and then only help will come.

I speak at last.

"He and I will face each other in single combat," I say, my voice steadier than I feel. "The winner will be chosen by Maat, the Spirit of Truth, Justice and Cosmic Order."

When I at last meet my wife's eyes, I am startled by the terror in them. I take her hands and lead her from the hall, the courtiers and soldiers moving back in stunned silence. I walk with confident dignity, as though I have no doubts about what I have just pronounced.

Merytaten, the royal queen she is, holds her head high and looks straight ahead. No one but I can feel how tightly her hand holds to mine.

When we are alone I tell her she must return to Akhetaten and her father's house, until the matter between Ma-nan and myself is settled.

"You cannot make me!" she cries defiantly. She is trembling violently, and she no longer holds back her tears.

"I can and I will," I say firmly.

"A prisoner?"

"If need be."

"I too will fight you, and Maat will be our judge!"

I can't help a smile at her small, fierce face, wet with tears. Furious she raises her fists to me, but I hold her wrists and she is helpless — until she remembers her feet. and she is helpless — until she remembers her feet.

When she is worn out I take her in my arms.

"This city is no place to be," I reason with her. "If I am not with you, you will be miserable and in danger. Ma-nan is not the only assassin."

"Why do you let him go?" she demands.

"I do not. Have you so little faith in me that you think that he will win?"

"You know he won't hesitate to use sorcery."

"I have known him all my life. He will not take me by surprise."

And then, because I can see the depth of her fears for me, I speak to her like an old man, wise in years, telling her that of course life is full of dangers, but none of them are random. . . . "A man can swim through a river full of crocodiles and come out unscathed. Another can stand in the safety of his own doorway and be killed by the falling of the lintel. Death will come only when we are ready for the next stage of life."

She listens to me, but I can see my words do not help her.

"Many people die suddenly, when they are not ready. Many people suffer when they don't deserve it. . . ."

"The readiness I speak of is not obvious to the ordinary eye, but only to the soul. Likewise, the suffering humans endure has reasons only the soul knows, sometimes punishments for deeds committed, sometimes lessons to be learned. . . ."

She shivers, although the summer heat of the sun is scorching the Two Lands and the air is visibly vibrating.

Ma-nan and I travel in silence. We cross the river to the

134

west bank, only the water speaking, and are escorted beyond the land of the living, beyond my father's mortuary temple with its colossal images in stone. There we are left to continue our journey alone, the soldiers staring after us in silence, puzzled no doubt by the orders they have been given.

We climb the mountains, pausing from time to time to draw breath and to look back over the landscape we have left behind, the green and fertile fields of barley and wheat, the pennants flying bravely from the temple pylons, the gleam of gold from the tall obelisks on the east bank: the teeming, fly-ridden, noisy life of the Pharaoh's people. My people. . . .

And then we are in an empty world. Dry rock, dry sand and dry sky. . . .

To the hawk soaring far above us we must be two moving specks. How could he suspect that in those minute dark spots on the vast, ochre-coloured earth, thoughts could take shape which are capable of making the entire universe as small as a mote in the eye?

The reality we had believed in, surrounded by the chattering minds of others, has long since fallen away, and, faced now by an immensity of silence, and left naked by the removal of the opinions, explanations and beliefs of others, we face a reality that has no compromises, no comforting padding of illusion. I have chosen the high desert deliberately, and the dawn is to see the beginning and the end of our duel.

We reach a plateau at sunset, and watch with awe as the huge red orb of the Aten disk sinks in the west. I don't know what prayer Ma-nan speaks in his silence, but my cry is to the one there is no word for, whose cipher, even, is too bright to gaze upon, who was and is and ever will be. . . . After the disk has left us there is a great hush. Silently the huge vault of the sky is suffused with red light, slowly spreading, slowly deepening. We watch as the night

135

shadow comes creeping over the desert to tug at the crimson mantle of the sky. We watch until the first stars appear. And then, when darkness has won, we settle on the bare earth to sleep, pulling our cloaks about us. I lie a long time on my back, looking up at the sky, feeling the earth wheel beneath me, the stars wheel above me. We give the stars names, we even identify them with our dead kings: we draw the pattern they make to us on papyrus or on stone, and give these patterns names of power: but who knows their real names, their real power: and who knows what part we play in those designs, and how we affect those who affect us?

The star of Isis, my star Sothis, is not visible. It will rise just before dawn, heralding the sun and the inundation. It is appropriate that Ma-nan and I should face each other at this time. It is the anniversary of my birth and of my first rebellion. Such marking of the cycles of earth time might not be very significant in the huge splendour of the great design, but without them earth-children are afraid.

I watch the stars' slow, slow movement across the heavens and prepare myself for the dawn. There are to be no physical weapons of any kind. This is a mind duel, a soul duel. I begin to be afraid, knowing Ma-nan's skill in mind-manipulation.

It is when my star rises, and only then, that I begin to feel confident. I have the living God and all the host of the beings of light to call upon, while his minions are lesser beings, failed souls and shadowy figments created by the dark side of himself.

He wakes, and I prepare the field.

I take the one object I have brought from Akhetaten, a crystal of total purity, a shaft of frozen light. I draw, on the loose sand that covers the ancient bedrock, a perfect circle, symbol of Ra's disk, the Aten, in turn symbol of that One which alone Is and to which all Other eventually returns.

Ma-nan watches me as a cat watches a mouse.

When I am done, and have spoken prayers to my god, I invite my enemy into the circle. The sun is rising, waves of its energy are beginning to touch everything into life.

Ma-nan steps confidently into the circle and stoops down instantly, to draw with his finger a five-pointed star, a pentagram, around himself, two of its points defiantly facing the sacred centre of the circle, duality, a gesture of obscenity to the One. Opposite him I draw another, this time one single point leading the eye to the centre of the circle. The sacred pentagram — the One, becoming the Two, becoming the Three. . . .

We stand within our two stars and look at each other. I know I should avoid his eyes: but if I do I cannot win, but only avoid the contest. I am no frightened child now, I tell myself, but an initiate and an adept as great as he, greater in many ways. It is not the time now to think of my failures and my weaknesses. I dare not doubt that I will win. After all he has no tricks of his trade with him, no resin that creates bad dreams, no amulets or charms, no figurines for sympathetic magic. But he has his mind — and he has his eyes.

I meet his gaze steadily, visualizing within my own mind as clearly as I can the brilliant disk of the sun, with the long rays of its energy reaching out, each ray terminating in a hand holding the ankh, the symbol of eternal life. I offer it to him without hate, but not yet with love.

He smiles, and the long rays become hissing snakes, the golden ankhs fall from the hands and become scorpions that race across the sand to me. At the centre of the Aten's disk I see a black spot, steadily growing larger as though the sun itself is diseased, like a rotten apple. For a moment I wonder if the dream we have of the pure light of the Aten giving understanding to all men's hearts is a false one, as corrupt as that which we strive to replace. For a moment I lose faith. For a moment I doubt.

Then I force myself not to run from the scorpions and

the snakes; force myself to destroy the visualization, and make my mind a blank.

I call to mind the gods of the Two Lands, carefully placing them where they belong, as aspects of the One, as Neters, named powers of the Great Spirit, limbs of the Great Body. Thoth, the teacher of wisdom, the opener of eyes. Ptah, the fashioner of shape and form. Osiris the resurrection. Hapi, the eternal river of Life. Maat, Truth and Justice, the sustainer of Order and Harmony. Hathor, the great Mother, the lady of intuition. Isis — ah, yes — Isis. . . .

As I call each name, and the attributes associated with it, I deliberately avoid visualizing, trying to disassociate the traditional image from the meaning behind the image: but the images have become too powerful, too set after millennia of depiction; and under Ma-nan's skilled direction they take form and howl around me in the circle, jackal-headed, lion-headed, scorpion-headed — subject, as images always are, to the corruption of he who conjures with them.

I cower like a green boy against their onslaught, over-whelmed by the strength of my enemy's mind, mocked by the fact that it was I who had called their names and thus called them into presence.

But this is sorcery, I tell myself, and sorcery though powerful cannot prevail against the strength of spirit. It is of the earth, subject to time and space, as fragile and transient as the earth itself.

I take a deep breath.

Beyond the false images is the horizon, not of the desert, but of the burning ring of fire my crystal-drawn circle has become. Within the circle the two lions, yesterday and tomorrow, past and future, crouch back-to-back. Between them, the present moment is poised, and in great danger. I step over that threshold with courage and am instantly No-where, No-time, and Ma-nan is without his protective demons.

Now I have the advantage, because as pilgrim seeking truth I have come this way before; but it is unfamiliar to him. The power he has trained himself to have is over things, and over people. He has sought for knowledge only that he may use it to increase his power over others. I have sought it for its own sake, and because it brings me nearer to the One from whom I come, and to whom I yearn to return.

I choose my weapon carefully. It is a dangerous one, and one for which I have to seek permission. It is the right to question a man about himself.

Khurahtaten takes me before the three Assessors who examine my motives, my emotions and my conscience. I am given permission, with the proviso that I am not to ask anything I would not be prepared to answer myself.

I look at Ma-nan, and he is there.

He seems to have grown in stature. He towers above me, magnificent in the robes of an adept, the inevitable symbols of his trade, the staff, the sphere, the feather. Behind him, rising like a thunder cloud, his god Amun, with eyes of fire burning into mine.

I cannot help but tremble. Do I sense that beyond him there are others, waiting? Are they waiting to see what the outcome will be, or waiting to take part in shaping the outcome?

If I win, I will defeat more than Ma-nan. If I lose, I will lose more than myself.

"Together," he says, "we will hold the Two Lands in our hands. It is ripe: we will pluck it and no one will have the strength to take it from us. Think of that, boy-with-no-name."

The old jibe still hurts. I fall for the trick, and try to assert my little ego.

"I have a name. Sothis. Smenkh-ka-Re, Beloved-of-the-Living-Aten. Beloved-of-Waenré-Akhenaten — "

"Beloved-of-Amun, chosen by him to lead the world back

to strength and health when the heretic is dead. The name he gives you will ring through eternity, and nations will tremble at the sound of it. If you stay with your dying prince you will be forgotten before the present generation of men has grown old, no trace of you will be found on earth, no memory of you will stir men's hearts. Your achievements will be accredited to others. The praises that should be yours will be sung to others. It will be as though you had never been."

I am afraid, but I pull myself together. How is it that I listen to what he says, knowing that the threats he uses are threats I should be using against him? But I haven't used them. I am silent, thinking of the power he promises me, the glory, the fame that will last until the world's end.

"Amun is generous to his friends," Ma-nan continues smoothly. "Did he not make his priests richer than the pharaoh? A pharaoh who honours him will be cased in gold when he departs this earth."

"And while he lives . . .?" I ask hoarsely.

"Gold and precious stones . . . spices and scents and women. . . . There will be nothing that he requests that will not be granted."

"Except his freedom," I whisper, more to myself than to him.

"*Freedom!*" shouts Ma-nan angrily. "What is greater freedom than being the ultimate power in the land, controlling the lives and deaths of every creature in the kingdom?"

My heart is like lead. "With the weight of all those lives and deaths on his breast, how can a man breathe?" I say.

"Ask your brother," he says sharply.

My brother? Myself? But we do not see ourselves as puppet-masters, as slayers of millions. We see ourselves as entrusted with a great task, we see ourselves as channels through which the waters of life flow from the source to the hidden grain. We are free in the sense that we have chosen this task, and we want to carry it through. In another sense we are not free, because the means we use to achieve it are dictated by the end we have in mind. We cannot choose to kill those who oppose us. I cannot choose to kill Ma-nan. For in doing so the means will corrupt the end, and nothing of what we want to achieve will be achieved. Freedom is a word more misunderstood than any other. But one thing I know is that there is no greater slavery than being a slave to one's own desires — whether it be for material possessions, for power, or, most insidious of all, for the good opinion and admiration of others.

"It is my turn to ask you a question, Ma-nan," I say now quietly, feeling my strength returning.

"Ask," he says boldly, confident that he has won the first round.

"Who is there who loves you, Ma-nan? Who has ever loved you?"

"*Loves* me!" he exclaims, caught off-balance by the unexpectedness of the question. He says the word "love" as though it is an obscenity.

"Whom have you loved, Ma-nan? Whom have you ever loved?"

His face twists, and for a moment I could swear his whole body visibly shrinks. He has never loved. Never been loved. Behind him I see that even Amun does not love him; nor does he love Amun. They use each other, but they do not love each other.

"Why has no one ever loved you?" I ask.

Will he blame others as he always has done, or will he look to his own blame?

"Why have you never loved?"

Will he know that it is because he has been afraid to give? Afraid to share? Wanting everything for himself?

How sad, how sad not to know even what love is. I do not want or expect him to give me answers. I want him only to examine his own heart. It seems that this is already happening,

141

because he is squatting on the ground now, his cloak like a pool of shadow around him, a frown between his eyes, his lips a tight line. The questioning continues. I cannot stop myself now. It is as though the questions are being asked through me, rather than by me.

"Have you ever done anything for anyone that is for their sake alone, and not for your own?

"Have you ever done anything for anyone that has made their lives better, happier, richer?"

"I have changed men's lives," he snarls. "I have changed many men's lives."

"For the better, or for the worse?"

"Why should I do anything for *them*?" he shouts. "What have they ever done for *me*?"

If you don't know the answer to this, I think, *there is no hope for you*.

"Whom have you hated? Who has hated you?"

Hate, he knows. I see his thoughts, and shudder at the shapes they take. Even Na-aghta, who might have been called "friend", distrusts, betrays: is distrusted, is betrayed. I see by his eyes that he is beginning to turn: beginning to regret: beginning to find the hate-feast sickening.

"Ask yourself why you hate," I whisper. "Why? Is it because in seeking self-respect you think it is easier to push everyone down below your own level, than to raise yourself up to theirs?

"The knowledge you have gained as initiate and adept," I say. "How have you used it?"

Here, for a moment, the old spark flares up, as he remembers the triumphs he has had using his knowledge.

But then the question comes: "Do you remember the law that governs the use of such knowledge? The law that forbids the use of it for harm, for the exploitation of others?" The expression of triumph leaves his face. He knows what law he has broken, and what the punishment will be.

He turns his head away from me. He is rocking backwards and forwards on the balls of his feet and his heels, hugging his knees. Behind him I can no longer see the image of his god. We are alone, and it is very silent.

There is one more question I have to ask before I am through: and it is one I myself would not like to answer.

"Have you ever heard a cry for help, and, it being in your power to help, not answered it?"

His hands are up, tearing at his face as though he would like to remove all the flesh of it and throw it away. The questioning has been no ordinary questioning. It has penetrated. It has hurt.

I sink down beside him and take his hands.

"Ma-nan," I say gently, "don't.... There is no need. What is past, is past. Come, look at me."

Compassion has warmed my heart towards him and, at that moment, witnessing his despair, I begin to see how it is possible for him to change, for our relationship to change. I no longer fear him. I see in him what might have been: what could still be.

I have won the duel with myself. Whether I have won the duel with him, only time and events will tell.

The rising sun sees two men seated in the desert; the young one with the old one's head resting on his shoulders.

The dawn breeze stirs the sand and removes all traces of the two pentagrams.

The circle remains.

No time passes in eternity.

The Death

I return to the city of the Aten, and am greeted at the quay as I step off the royal boat by one of my lector priests, white-faced and shaking. He tries to draw me aside, whispering incoherently that there is danger, and we must leave at once. But to do so is impossible. Already officials are crowding me, and I am caught up in the elaborate greeting ceremonial. But there is something wrong. I can see it in the eyes of the men who bow before me. I can see it in the faces of the crowds that the guards are holding back. I look around for the friend who tried to warn me, but he is now nowhere in sight. Is it my imagination or am I being treated differently from usual?

As I climb into my golden chariot, and acknowledge the muted greeting of the young groom who holds the reins, I know that there is something that no one wants to tell me. I wind the reins around my hand, and steady my feet on the unstable wicker floor as the horse tramples the ground uneasily. Haughtily, from this height, I demand an explanation. I note the looks that pass between the men before one has the courage to step forward and speak. Impatiently I wait through the long preamble protocol demands, until I get to the nub of the answer — and then I go cold. It is as though all light has been extinguished.

The king is dead.

"An illness," they murmur. "Suddenly . . . without warning . . . only a few hours ago. . . ."

I can see by their faces that this is what they have been told — but not what they believe. It seems they had intended to keep the news from me until we reached the palace. There has been no official announcement and the people are not yet aware of what has happened, though rumours have already begun to fly around.

As I gallop through the streets towards the palace I see nothing of the city around me. My heart is pounding with the name of my brother, but the reality of his death has not yet fully penetrated.

I find the palace heavily guarded by Horemheb's men. The general had not been expected in the city when I left. Yet he is here now. There is no doubt in my mind that he is somehow responsible for my lord's death. I also have no doubt that he will be responsible for mine if I do not take care. My skin prickles when I think about him. A strong man, always watching, biding his time. He has always disapproved of everything we believe in, and I know that if he could he would reinstate the old ways. To him, religion is entirely an exoteric affair: a matter of words and rituals, performed to reinforce the ancient grid of order that has held the people quiet and docile for millennia. He supports Amun-Ra because the priests of Amun-Ra support the army and the army is the pharaoh's strong arm. Without fear of a pharaoh with a strong arm, he believes a land will fall into anarchy, and it is surely this fear that motivates him now. I respect him enough to believe that whatever he has done he believes it is for the good of the Two Lands. The trouble is — he sees only the body of the Two Lands, not the spirit.

Within the palace the wailing of mourners is already mounting to a crescendo. Akhenaten's harem of secondary wives are beating their fists against the door of his chamber and against their own breasts, the cosmetics they have used on their faces streaking their cheeks with black and green. I am admitted at once to the presence of General Horemheb. Beside him is the Princess Nezem-mut with her two dwarfs. There is no sign of her sister Nefertiti. Horemheb is issuing orders to a group of officials gathered around him, and a few moments pass before he notices me. When he does, he breaks away from the people who surround him.

"My lord," he says, "Pharaoh of the Two Lands, Lord of the Thresholds and Mighty Bull of Men-Nefer!" He prostrates himself, his forehead on the tiled floor, among the marsh scenes and lotus flowers. His action is followed by everyone in the room; Ay wheezing as he lowers his frame to the floor. I gesture that Nefertiti's father should rise.

"It is not necessary that a man so rich in years and honours, father of divinity, Bearer of the Fan on the right hand of the king, Acting Scribe of the king and beloved by him, Overseer of all the horses of his Majesty and head of his companions, should stay so low," I say — but the others I keep down for some moments longer. Seeing their prostrate forms shocks me. I know now that I am indeed pharaoh. As regent, the bow required had not been so low, nor were they expected to stay down until I gave them leave to rise.

At last I release them and they scramble to their feet, Horemheb red in the face with annoyance, knowing that I have deliberately kept him down longer than necessary and also given him no precedence over the others.

All look to me now for instruction.

Time in that room seems to stand still as I gradually adjust to the realization that my friend, my brother, is indeed dead. Pain begins to come to my hitherto numb heart, a lump to my throat. Huskily I ask to be escorted to my king, and that the physician who had been attending him be brought to me. I am told that his own physician is away from the city, and Horemheb's army physician had attended him. I demand the presence of the second court physician. It seems he, too, is away. I discover that all the men who had been closest to the king, his friends, his favourites, are mysteriously away from the city. I remember bitterly that I, too, was not there when he needed me.

"Has the Queen Nefertiti been informed?" I ask. *Was she dead, too?* I am speaking calmly, coldly, but my heart is beating so loudly with my secret fears it is as though my voice is coming from far away.

Horemheb meets my eyes steadily. His face is expressionless.

"The Queen Nefertiti and her daughters are in the northern palace, my lord, under guard for their own safety. I have to inform you that the queen is under suspicion of having poisoned her husband."

Is this possible? *Is it?* I look at Nezem-mut standing behind Horemheb. Her face is drawn and miserable. I meet her eyes and know that she is as afraid as I am. She recognizes my question, and moves her head almost imperceptibly. I am assured that she, at least, does not think her sister is to blame. They have never been close as sisters, but I suspect Nezem-mut would know if Nefertiti were guilty of such a deed.

"I do not believe that, sir," I say coldly. "The queen loved her husband."

"The queen is ambitious."

"If to be ambitious puts one under suspicion of murder, General, then you yourself would be under suspicion."

I tremble as I say this, but am glad that I have the courage.

His expression does not change. He stares steadily into my eyes.

"And you, my lord."

I can feel the tension in those around us. I can almost

147

hear the crack of the soldiers' knuckles as they tighten their grip on their weapons. I could point out that I was not in the palace when the king took ill, but that he was, but I know and he knows I will not say this. I, and all who loved Akhenaten, are in great danger.

I turn to the door of the king's bed-chamber, and with some semblance of authority indicate that the people crowding round it should be sent away. The mourners move, but I notice his soldiers stand their ground until Horemheb gives the sign.

I pass through the door panelled in ebony and ivory, and enter the chamber, almost overpowered as I do so by the smell of incense. My friend is on his bed, laid out on his back, his hands folded on his chest. I stand beside him looking down. The embalmers have not touched him yet, but he is already as stiff as a statue. I hate the thought of their cutting into him, of their pulling out his viscera, his brain, his heart.

"Will you not speak to me, my friend?" I whisper. But he does not reply — and a terrible loneliness fills my heart. *What will become of me?* I wonder. *Am I in a position to do anything? to make any decision?*

Horemheb is treating me with careful outward respect, as though he acknowledges that I am king; but I know he does not fear me as I fear him. If I make one wrong move, I am a dead man.

My heart aches for my poor friend, lying so still. He was a great man; a dreamer, a believer, a reacher after the numinous essence of the world . . . and now he is an object lying helplessly at the mercy of the servants of Anubis, who are already gathering in the palace, bringing their jars of natron and their polished knives.

I turn from his side, and ask in a low voice for my wife. Nezem-mut takes my hand.

"She is with her mother," she says quietly.

"Release her!" I cry, suddenly rounding on Horemheb.

"By what authority do you hold my queen prisoner?"

"She is not a prisoner, my lord," he answers smoothly. "She chose of her own accord to be with her mother, and is free to leave her side at any time."

"What proof have you that Nefernefruaten Nefertiti has done this deed?" I demand, indicating the still figure on the bed.

He purses his lips. "It is not proven, my lord, it is suspected."

"On what grounds?"

"It is known that they have been estranged lately. It is known that she covets the double crown herself."

"Who knows this, General? *I* do not know this!"

He shrugs.

"In your absence, my lord, I thought it best to confine her to her palace until more is known about the circumstances of the king's death."

"Send for Nefernefruaten Nefertiti, the princesses and my queen," I say coldly.

"With respect, my lord . . ." Horemheb begins.

"Send for them," I repeat firmly. I am thinking: If I go to them I may be trapped in that northern palace. This one is larger, more open. It will not be so easy to guard and is not too far from the quay if we need to leave in a hurry.

Unwillingly the general gives the order. It seems that for the moment, at least, he has decided to accept me as pharaoh.

I go to the throne-room to await their arrival, watched by soldiers, struggling to keep the violence of my emotions under control. I feel I am walking on an eggshell floor over a bottomless pit.

I sit in my brother's great chair, and grip the arms of it until the muscles in my own arms ache. I look straight ahead as though I am already a statue frozen in stone to stare dispassionately into the lives of future generations. Where is my brother? Where? I cannot feel him near me. It is as if he has never been.

I must keep control of myself. I must. If they see that I am afraid I will lose everything. To the people, by becoming pharaoh, I have taken on the mantle of the god. My strength, my calm must sustain them all. There were many things my brother did that I did not totally approve of and many things I thought I could do better if I were pharaoh. Well, now I am pharaoh. Sickeningly my heart thuds. Now I am pharaoh. The thought terrifies me. It is not only fear of Horemheb. It is fear of myself.

By the time the women are brought before me I am in control of myself. I have called for Akhenaten's royal golden cobra to be fitted to my crown, and feel stronger under its protection. I have made enquiries of those who attend me and learned that many of Akhenaten's closest supporters have fled the city, and gone into hiding, some talking of leaving the country altogether. Officially there is no talk of assassination, but there is no doubt in anyone's mind that that is exactly what it was. No one knows for sure who is responsible. I can sense that our friends are convinced it was done on Horemheb's command, though nothing is said to that effect. Horemheb's supporters, on the other hand, are loud in their accusation against Akhenaten's queen.

She walks into the throne-room as light as a feather, her head held high, her blue crown giving her a height she does not naturally have. Her beauty, even after the bearing of six children, is astonishing. Behind her come her daughters, Ankhesenpaaten looking tired and sullen, the young ones terrified, clinging to their mother; Merytaten, my beloved, walking slightly apart from them, her face drawn and dark as though she has been weeping incessantly since I left her. When she sees me her soul flies to me, and although our bodies are separate, we are together.

Akhenaten had broken with tradition in placing a throne for his queen, his Great Royal Wife, on the same level and of the same size as his own. In statues and in paintings she was usually beside him and not behind, and in real life she was treated with equal respect.

I am momentarily at a loss, overwhelmed by the majesty of her presence, uncertain whether to indicate that she should sit beside me in her usual chair, or keep her standing in front of me. Rightfully, the second throne is now Merytaten's. Our eyes meet, and she reads my mind as though it is a papyrus laid out on a scribe's knee. Without hesitation Akhenaten's queen prostrates herself before me. I can hear the gasp that goes round the hall. The children are bewildered and shocked, not knowing if they should follow suit. Ankhesenpaaten looks disgusted and holds her ground. Merytaten, perhaps more to hide her tears which have started flowing again at sight of me than to make obeisance, falls down beside her mother. This is too much. I leap up and stoop to raise them both. I do not care that Horemheb has entered, his sombre eyes taking in the whole scene.

"Beloved of Neferkhepruré Waenré, there is no need. . . ."

"Am I not accused, my lord, as a common criminal?" she says proudly, her falling and her rising accomplished with equal grace.

"Not by me," I say quickly. "Not by me."

"The king has just returned to the city," Horemheb says sharply, moving forward. "He has no knowledge of the events that led up to this sorry day."

"Who shall enlighten him, General," Nefertiti says haughtily, "you or I?"

"I will find out the truth by my own methods, in my own time," I say sternly, "but I am interested to hear what each of you has to say."

I solve the problem of the thrones by calling servants to provide chairs for the royal party, and for Horemheb, and arrange them in a circle, so that no one can tell who is or is not being honoured or disgraced. The soldiers and the servants are sent away, so that they will not hear what is said. Nurses are called for the youngest princesses, and they too are removed.

I let Horemheb speak first, knowing the advantage is always with the one who has the last word.

I am aware of the fierce, penetrating eyes of the cobra on my forehead, and find myself believing that it is not I who am seeing and listening and judging, but the piercing eyes of the past pharaohs, the mighty god-kings who built the pyramids and are held in a continuing dialogue with the Two Lands as long as their mortuary rituals last, as long as their tombs contain the ancient holding spells. The golden band around my head burns, and I feel as though the top of my head has floated off and is hovering above me, the eye of fire seeing into the very souls of Horemheb and Nefertiti.

He speaks carefully, his words picked and chosen with great skill. He had come to Akhetaten, he tells me, to plead with his king once more for help on the eastern frontier. Vassal kings were rising against vassal kings and to keep the peace and protect the pharaoh's interests in the east, Horemheb needed more troops, more weapons, more supplies. He claims that Akhenaten agreed to give him these things the night before he died. He claims also that it is Nefertiti who had made the king weak, turning his heart away from the empire his forefathers had won for him, seducing him with music and art, and encouraging him in his heretical policy, suicidal for the country, of destroying the stable network of belief in local gods under the central control of Amun-Ra. He claims that it was when she realized Akhenaten had at last woken up to the fact that he had to defend his empire, and had agreed to give Horemheb the men and weapons he needed, and that she was losing control of him, that she decided to murder him, and take the throne herself.

I look at her closely. Her skin is like alabaster, her eyes

lapis lazuli. I cannot read her face. It is too beautiful, too composed. But my cobra eye looks into her heart. I know she supported and encouraged her husband in everything he did up to the death of their daughter Maketaten. But at her death a change had come over her, over them both. There is no denying that they had their differences, but I had not thought Nefertiti had veered so far from their original goal that she would even contemplate the deed of which she now stands accused.

"Speak," I say to her, and take Merytaten's hand, knowing that she is near to breaking point.

Nefertiti turns her head and looks into the eyes of Horemheb. He meets hers steadily at first, and then shifts uneasily in his seat, lowering his eyes. She smiles very slightly and turns to me.

"You are pharaoh," she says softly. "You can see into men's hearts. You need no words from me to teach you the truth."

"*I* need no words," I say, "but the General. . . . *He* needs words."

Are we allies now against a greater evil, she and I who have had our differences, our jealousies? The man we loved is dead. My hand tightens on Merytaten's. If it were not for her, my loneliness would be unendurable. If it were not for her, my desire for Akhenaten's widowed queen would be irresistible. I look at Horemheb, wondering about his feelings. Nefertiti looks at us both, knowing what she knows.

Ankhesenpaaten, older than her years, speaks up suddenly. "It seems to me," she says coldly, "this questioning has no point to it. My lord, the king is dead. There was no mark of violence on him, no drop of poison lingering on his lips. Why do we fruitlessly accuse my mother of murder? He was not a healthy man. Anyone could see that. He died. Let that be an end of it."

Has she no love for her father-husband, this aged child,

153

this pawn in the royal game? I am thankful Merytaten and I have married for love, though our marriage is also politically necessary. How different the two sisters are. How gentle Merytaten: how hard her sister. I pray that I will not drive my wife to bitterness, and I fight the thought that slyly comes to me, that to marry Nefertiti and make her co-regent with myself will be to keep something of Akhenaten alive upon the throne. The thought itself has merit, but the motive . . . the hidden motive comes from my secret desire, and has nothing to do with my belief as to what is good for the country. I release Merytaten's hand, afraid that she will "feel" my duplicity.

"General, your accusations are far-fetched. This ambition of which you speak. . . . How can the lady 'take' the throne? Pharaoh lives," I say haughtily.

"A man may die," he replies coolly, "and there may be no mark of violence on him, no drop of poison lingering on his lips."

I am silent.

Merytaten suddenly stands up, her face flushed with anger.

"You go too far!" she cries. "My mother *loved* my father! Loves Sothis now as friend and brother!"

"Your mother offered *me* the double crown," Horemheb says drily, looking hard at the widowed queen.

For a moment her composure falters and it seems my heart stops beating. Merytaten gasps and stands bewildered, not knowing whether to hit Horemheb in the face for insulting her mother or to spit in her mother's face for what she now feels is almost certain betrayal of her father. Being Merytaten she does neither, but in her eyes I see the dawning of a great pain. She has not realized before, this protected child of the City of the Sun, how complex and dangerous life can be even among one's own family. Her sister has, and is listening now to every word with close attention, apparently unperturbed and unsurprised by what she hears.

154

I feel as though I have suddenly fallen through that floor of eggshell on which I was so precariously balanced.

Should I abdicate now, and leave the double crown to those who so desire it that they will cheat and kill for it? Suddenly I am tired and long to walk beside the lake at Per-hay talking with my friend. Let Nefertiti marry Horemheb and rule the Two Lands. . . .

I do not realize how unquestioningly I have believed Horemheb until I hear Nefertiti reply to him.

"You lie, General," she says, with a deadly stillness in her voice, reminding me of the stillness of a snake before it strikes. "I offered you my body — not the crown."

The silence is almost tangible.

For me the courage of the queen in saying this has convinced me utterly that Horemheb is the one who is lying. A dark stain of anger floods his face, his lips move, but no sound is emitted. For the first time I feel almost sorry for him. I can see that he genuinely believed that she had offered him the crown, and that all that he had done was in this expectation. It is probable that when she withheld what he thought his right, he turned on her and tried to destroy her. I realize also how tenuous my own hold on the crown, and on life, has been these last days. His disappointment in her is the only thing that has kept me alive.

The tension is broken by Merytaten, who becomes hysterical and starts to cry and scream and beat her fists against her mother. Nezem-mut, who has been sitting silently and uneasily beside Horemheb all this while, thinking her own thoughts, moves forward swiftly and helps me drag her niece away. Nefertiti remains unmoved, standing straight and proud, challenging Horemheb with her eyes, Ankhesenpaaten watching them both with a kind of unhealthy fascination.

When Merytaten is calm at last, and I can turn my attention

back to the others, Horemheb has left. Nefertiti is sitting on the edge of her throne, her face buried in her hands, sobbing painfully. I leave Merytaten in the arms of Nezemmut, and stand before Akhenaten's queen. My urge to take her in my arms, now that she is weeping, is very strong.

"Nefernefruaten Nefertiti," I say softly, "I accuse you of nothing. You are free to go where you will: but I hope you will choose to stay with me, and help me through these dark days."

Does she hear me through her sobs? She gives no sign. I stand silently in front of her, my hands hanging at my sides awkwardly, waiting. At length the sobs die down, and she raises her face to mine.

"If we could only go back," she murmurs sadly, "back to before it all went wrong. There are things I would do that I did not do then, and things that I would not do now. . . ."

My arms do not touch her, but my eyes hold her with great compassion and love.

"I used to hate you," she says, looking at me wonderingly, "because he seemed to want to spend more time with you than with me."

"I used to hate you," I say, "because there were things he shared with you he would not share with me."

At this moment I know for the first time that my love for Akhenaten was also desire, and that my desire for her is also love.

Merytaten touches my arm. She has heard everything we have said — and not said.

Events move very swiftly in the next few days.

I am pharaoh, but I find that every order I give has been pre-empted by Horemheb. He has real control of the country, while I have nominal control. I contemplate overthrowing him and seizing power myself, but I can see that I have not the strength to do it. He has been expanding the army over the past few years, using his own fortune

156

when Akhenaten would not give him help, and now has
what is virtually a private army. The displaced priests of
Amun have aided him, and most of the considerable riches
of their temples, which should have come directly to the
king for use in his building programme, have found their
way to Horemheb.

I realize that my only hope for personal survival, and for
the survival of Akhenaten's family and ideals, is for me to
appear to acquiesce in Horemheb's plans, while watching
closely for an opportunity to subvert them. In the affairs of
the world, when you do not have physical power you have
to learn cunning.

Merytaten is shocked that I appear so docile. I do not
accuse Horemheb openly of having brought about the
death of Akhenaten, and he in his turn drops his accusations
against the widow-queen. We both pretend to the nation
that the king died of natural causes. As Ankhesenpaaten
said, he was not a robust man, and to die suddenly of an
illness is not unknown. That all his closest friends apart
from Ay and myself have disappeared is known, but not
commented on too loudly by those left at court.

Ay is a great help to us and it is he who persuades
Merytaten that the waiting game is best. A man who was
much respected by Akhenaten's father, he is also respected
by Horemheb. He is the bridge over which I cross when I
want to placate the powerful general. It is Ay who helps me
persuade Horemheb that it would cause more harm than
good to declare the king publicly a heretic and reverse all
his decrees at once. I speak of gradual change as I did to my
brother, but this time I am more successful. The ban is
lifted on the priests of Amun, but the Aten temples still
flourish. I hope to make the worship of the Aten a deeper
and more natural thing, stressing that it is the purest
expression of the One God as yet known to man, comple-
menting and completing the other images and conceptions
we already have. I know that people are apt to seize one or

two of the most comprehensible elements in any faith, and elevate these to a status they do not deserve. Whether they will understand the subtlety of what I am trying to communicate, I am by no means sure, but it seems the only path to tread, with Horemheb breathing down my neck to reinstate Amun-Ra, and Merytaten looking at me with big accusing eyes whenever I appear to be deserting the letter of her father's beliefs.

The tomb Ay has been preparing for himself, in the valley east of Akhetaten, already has exquisite representations of Akhenaten and his family under the protective rays of the Aten. He now orders the artists to discreetly introduce the other gods.

Akhenaten's funeral arrangements have been taken out of my hands. Whenever I approach the chambers where the embalmers are working I am turned aside, politely but firmly, by one or other of the guards. I am drawn, by a need I cannot explain to myself, to ride out over the hot sands to his tomb.

At the entrance to the valley that breaks into the eastern range I rein in, and decide to walk the rest of the way to the royal tomb; the clatter of the horse's hooves and the rattle of the chariot wheels on the loose pebbles annoys me. I feel I need silence, I need to think.

Once out of range of my horse's gentle snorting as he crops the sparse, prickly vegetation, I have silence indeed. In some places I walk on rock and between high, hard cliffs, and have the uncanny experience of hearing the echo of my own footsteps, but for the most part I walk on soft sand and hear nothing. The funeral procession of Maketaten had come this way, and her father's will be following soon. Occasionally, I fancy I hear Hathor's silver sistrum being shaken, and a brief burst of chanting; but faint and insubstantial, as though it is but the memory of the past haunting these still mountains, waiting to be used again. I must remember, I tell myself, to notice whether Akhenaten's music is all his own, or whether there is some ghost music closely mingled with it.

Narrow valleys, roughly carved out by storm water, lead off the broad processional way, some overshadowed by pyramidal rocks, others having no distinguishing sign. I know which one to take, and stand before the entrance to my brother's tomb. Who would know from the outside that this crude hole in the rock hid so much?

I stoop and enter. It lies as it was at the moment of his death — unfinished — tools lying where workmen have dropped them, the rock silent and brooding.

I walk down the long corridor where I had floated once with Khurahtaten. There is a terrible emptiness, a feeling of desolation. I feel again what I felt the day of his death. It is as though he has never been.

I stand in the chamber where his sarcophagus should eventually lie, and I begin to feel a strange and heady drowsiness. There is a faint lingering smell of incense, from the time he and Nefertiti tried to practise their magic rites, but this could not induce what I am feeling now.

I sit down beside the wall and lean my head back against the cold surface. I can feel myself drifting off to sleep and cannot stop myself. Gradually I notice that the darkness I had fallen into is lifting, and I am standing on a rock surveying a desert landscape. The sun is a burning hole in the sky, the land shimmering and insubstantial. Above my head vultures are circling. I stare into the glare, trying to see what is drawing their attention. There is a dark smudge on the sand. From this distance I cannot be sure what it is. There is an icy feeling in my heart as I walk over the scorching sands towards the shape. I know, somehow, what I will find.

Buckled and broken on the sand I find the body of a man, already stripped by the scavengers of the desert, yet still recognizable to my spirit-sight as my brother Akhenaten. A dark and malevolent shadow envelops him, and I know

159

that a spell has been cast to hold him to this place.

I tremble with rage. Is it not enough that they have murdered his body, that they have to deny him his chances in the after-life as well? As it is there will be no elaborate burial for him, no prayers to take him safely to his god, no place on earth where his soul may be made welcome so that future generations might benefit from his guidance and protection. Even a ghost tied to his once-earthly habitation, ceaselessly remembering the moment of his death, has the chance of exorcism and release. But here — who will find my brother? Who will set him free from this desolate place? I know it will not be long before they will hack out his name from all his monuments, and then it will be as though he has never been. . . .

I wake, shuddering, and find myself in his empty tomb.

I hurry away from the place, driving my light chariot swiftly back to the city. I see Merytaten and her sisters in the garden of the palace, but ignore them. I rush up the steps, along the corridors, through the halls, until I reach the chambers of the embalmers. There, I break through the restraining hands of the guards and fling open the door. On the slab, where the body of my brother should be lying, is nothing. The embalmers are sitting around drinking beer and talking, and look up with astonishment at my precipitate intrusion. In one blinding second I know that my dream was a true vision. Akhenaten's body is not being prepared for burial. The elaborate series of coffins that will be carried in procession to his tomb, and eventually lowered into his sarcophagus, will be empty. No *ka* is expected to inhabit the House of the Threshold through the long ages.

My brother is utterly doomed, and I with him.

It is at this moment I decide to make Nefertiti my co-regent; Ankhkheprure Nefernefruaten. We are both beloved of Akhenaten and his god. I cannot face what there is to face alone, and Merytaten is too young and too innocent to help me.

The Double Crown

Horemheb and the country accept for the time being that Nefertiti and I are pharaoh, Merytaten queen, Great Royal Wife: but there is not a day in which Nefertiti and I sit easy on the throne, or Merytaten lies peacefully in my bed.

I am offered other wives, and diplomacy dictates that I should give them a place in my household, but many of them are spies planted by Horemheb and the priests of Amun, and I find that there is no such thing as privacy, even in the inmost chambers of my palace.

I try to challenge Horemheb about the disappearance of Akhenaten's body, but am lied to so plausibly by the embalmers and the guards that I am made to look a fool for doubting that the carefully-fashioned set of coffins contains his remains. I am even shown a bandaged figure with each costly royal amulet in place, but by this time, of course, the corpse is unrecognizable.

The funeral goes ahead with the usual elaborate ritual, the final feast taking place inside the tomb as is customary, so that Akhenaten can take his leave of us as he would if he were going on a long journey. Nefertiti, Merytaten and I sit in the chairs of honour, garlanded with flowers, our beloved's effigy propped up beside us. Food and drink is passed for him, and the pretence kept up that he is present. Even the ceremony of the Opening of the Mouth is

161

performed before the coffins are lowered into the sarcophagus, that his soul may be empowered to communicate
with those in the otherworld, and with those left behind in
this. I look at Horemheb's expressionless face, and wonder
that he has so little faith in the gods he purports to
champion that he may mock their rituals so.

O my love, my friend, where are you? If I could find your broken
body perhaps I could at least avert some of the harm done
to you, by giving you a proper burial. Nefertiti is highly
skilled in magic — it may be that she can help with this.

The wine is heady, Merytaten's cheeks are flushed, her
eyes too bright. I feel so dizzy I wonder if it is drugged, and
whether it is intended that we never leave this tomb. The
singing of the young girls with blue lotus flowers in their
hair is very sweet, but seems very far away. . . .

When we wake we are back in the palace. So we are needed
alive a while longer? I feel each moment I live is only by the
grace of the stern general. Everyone around me seems to
be waiting for something to happen. Everyone is afraid.

As the days go by I try to placate Horemheb, allowing the
Amun priesthood certain rights again, opening temples
that had long been shut. I try not to think of my poor
brother, and how I betray him at every turn. Merytaten
begins to turn from my touch, and I read in her eyes that
she despises me for not seizing the power that is my right,
and using it. She also knows her mother's beauty has
seduced me, and watches bitterly as I flounder helplessly in
my desire for Nefernefruaten and in my fear of Horemheb.
When I can think clearly at all, which is not often, I am
shocked that I have abandoned all I have learned from
Khurahtaten. No wolf trap is a stronger snare than the
body's fears and desires. My brother's eyes haunt me. I tell
myself my pursuit of Nefertiti is for what she knows, not
for her beauty, and I watch for an opportunity to be with
her alone. It is not easy to escape the reproachful gaze of

Merytaten, or the net of Horemheb's spies, but at last we manage it. By trick and subterfuge we slip away and push out a boat on to the lake at Meru-Aten.

Nefertiti is marked by the strain of the past year. In her statues and her paintings she will always be beautiful, and her beauty will live for ever, but in the flesh now her beauty is tinged with a hardness and a gauntness that was not there in her youth. She looks at me in a way I do not like, seeing into my thoughts. She waits for me to speak first.

I hold myself back, careful not to touch her, careful to look straight ahead over the water to the small island in the centre of the lake, fringed with reeds, the home of Akhenaten's favourite rare breeds of waterfowl.

"Nefernefruaten," I say at last, "I have something to tell you that will hurt."

"Tell me," she says quietly.

I tell her for the first time about my scrying dream and then what I know of the fake funeral. I dare not look at her face, knowing what she must be feeling.

After what seems a long silence she says that she had not felt his presence at the funeral, and so is not surprised to hear what I have just told her.

It is a relief to speak about my experience, to share the burden of it. I cannot see her face because her back is now turned to me, but she remains upright and there is no sign that she is weeping. I am strengthened by her strength.

"You are versed in magic," I say. "Do you know a way of finding him?"

She is silent a long time.

"He forbade my magic," she says, in a low and bitter voice. "It would be an irony to use it now to save him."

"I don't ask it lightly."

She looks at me with those marvellous eyes, turning her head suddenly, my hands beginning to tremble as though the look she gives me is a touch.

163

"I will try," she says finally, "but I would be surprised if whoever did that to him did not also put on a spell against his finding."

Na-aghta would have done that, I think, on Horemheb's command. Ma-nan probably knows about it. Perhaps that is where I should start. But if he doesn't — or if he is back under Na-aghta's influence in spite of my winning the duel. . . .

That Na-aghta and Horemheb have left myself and Nefertiti alive, to rule, seems more and more sinister to me. They must be sure of their influence on us. They must be sure they have us trapped. For a few moments I despair; and then a duck lands on the surface of the lake throwing up a spray of silver water, which blazes suddenly in the sunlight. I am momentarily dazzled, and then my vision clears. Hiding-spell or no hiding-spell I will find Akhenaten's body, and ensure that its soul is free and safe to embark on its journey in the boat of millions of years. I only hope there will be someone to do the same for me if the need should arise.

Nefertiti and I spend a great deal of time together, not only dealing with our official duties under the watchful eyes of Horemheb and his spies, but also in seeking secretly for a magic spell that will give us the whereabouts of Akhenaten's body. Merytaten is very much aware of the way things are drifting, and retires more and more to her own chambers, making excuses that she is not feeling well, even when I do manage to visit her. I can feel the sadness in her and I fight it, telling myself that she is being unreasonable — there is nothing between her mother and myself but concern for the good of the Two Lands, and for Akhenaten's soul. I know I am lying to myself, but I continue nevertheless.

I try to win the friendship of Ay, for I suspect he has never really liked me, and still hankers to place his protégé Tutankhaten on the throne. The boy is growing rapidly, and I can see that if I am not careful we could be displaced by him. I make public declaration of my relationship to Sitamon, in spite of my brother's wish to keep it hidden, and stress Merytaten's claim to the royal blood-line.

I invite Tutankhaten to live with me in the palace, thinking that in this way I will be able to keep track of everyone he sees and knows. I have learned the value of spies from Horemheb. But Ay prevents his coming, telling me blandly that the boy is not well and cannot travel. He is resting in his father's palace at Per-hay.

Next I hear that Merytaten is ill. When I break down her chamber door at last I find her being delivered of a stillborn child, her women around her, and her sister Ankhesen-paaten holding her head. The anger with which this latter looks at me almost freezes my blood. I push aside the restraining arms of the women and fall down on my knees beside my beautiful child-wife. The pain she has been through has aged her.

I put my head on her breast and sob. Her hands take my head and stroke it, her voice whispers words of comfort. Once again it is *she* who apologizes for *my* cruelty, it is she who needs comfort, who comforts me. Ankhesenpaaten's face is distorted with bitterness. She deliberately spits on me. I hear Merytaten chiding her, and ordering her to leave the room. She starts to leave angrily, and then stoops down and picks up the dead and bloody foetus from the basin in which it is resting. Horrified, I look up to see her holding it high above me before she furiously dashes it to the ground.

"May you and all your offspring be cursed!" she screams, and runs out of the room.

I turn to Merytaten.

She has fainted.

I insist that Ankhesenpaaten leaves the city. She does so willingly, taking her entourage of women with her, going, on Ay's suggestions, to Per-hay to join her father's child-brother, Tutankhaten. She does not even say goodbye to her mother, believing perhaps, as her sister Merytaten does, that we are lovers as well as joint-pharaoh.

I almost forget the dangerous position I am in, and the urgency of my mission to find Akhenaten's body, in my desperation to make it up to Merytaten for the way I have been neglecting her. She and I become inseparable again, and are seen even in public locked in embrace, as Nefertiti and her husband once had been. There is an ominous quiet in the affairs of the country for a while, and I almost begin to believe my policy of careful compromise is working and that we will win through to a kind of peace.

Nefertiti now keeps away from me as much as possible, and although this pains me it is obviously a relief as well. I do not want to see her face, so like her daughter's, yet so strong and subtle in comparison; her figure still tantalizingly seductive in almost transparent pleated robes. I am determined to love Merytaten as I used to love her. I *do* love Merytaten. But increasingly I know my love for her is not enough. I need Nefertiti. There are things I can share with the woman, that I cannot share with the girl.

Forgive me, I cry silently, as I kiss the young girl's hair and neck and lips, as I touch her nipples with my tongue and feel my way into her body. *Forgive me that with every touch I think of Nefer-nefru-aten Nefert-iti. . . .*

If Merytaten knows what I am thinking, she gives no sign. Outwardly, everything between us looks well and she talks of another child, an heir for the double crown. It is only at night when she cannot sleep she remembers her sister's curse — and trembles.

One night I receive a message that my co-regent, Nefertiti, wishes to see me in her chamber. She has been absent from the great hall and the council chambers all day, and I hurry to her, wondering if she too has fallen ill.

She is on her couch when I enter, and her women silently slide away, leaving us alone. The lamplight flickers warmly

166

on her bare shoulders. A wrap as insubstantial as a spider's web lies across the rest of her body. I stand beside her, looking down at her. I feel as though I am at a cliff edge, deciding whether to leap off or not. I am not sure if it is an illusion of the lamplight or a real smile that flutters briefly on her lips. I can hold myself back no longer, and stoop to take her in my arms.

I cannot believe I have never done this in all the years I have known her. It seems now so natural, so inevitable.

When it is finished we lie silently for a long time, watching the light and shadow play on the painted ceiling, the canopy of flowers and leaves and birds depicted there.

"Why?" I ask at last. "Why now?"

She shrugs and draws her wraps around her as though she is cold.

"I had a fearful dream. I was afraid," she says.

I hold her close; these are uncertain and dangerous times. My dreams are fearful too.

"And now?" I ask. "Are you less afraid?"

She kisses me long and deeply, but she does not answer.

If anything, I am thinking, I am more afraid than I was before. We can both feel it, the violence just under the surface, the darkness that will not be held back for long.

"Did Horemheb — ?" I want to ask her outright if she and Horemheb had ever been lovers. I am afraid of the answer, but I want to know. I tell myself I need to know, for, knowing, I will be able to deal with him more easily.

She puts her slender finger on my mouth and stops the question before it is spoken.

"You asked me to find Wa-en-ré," she says. "Have you forgotten?"

"No," I say quickly, but I know I had forgotten — this night at least.

I rest on my elbow, looking down into her face, my own shading it from the lamplight. Her eyes are dark pools, her thoughts unfathomable.

167

"Have you found him?" I ask.

She shakes her head. "I cannot," she says. "My magic is not strong enough. I am certain now there is a very powerful hiding-spell on him."

I lie beside her, and we no longer touch. The memory of Akhenaten lies between us like a sword.

After a while I stand up and return to my own chambers, infinitely sad.

The Second Duel

When Horemheb leaves to attend to a sudden crisis else-
where, I seek out Ma-nan, and persuade him to help me
find the body of Akhenaten. I was right. He does know
where it is, and, although he resists at first, I have the
power now to make him submit. He has aged beyond belief
since I have last seen him, even his skin looks grey and he
shakes continually. It seems his evil genius was his only
strength, and without it he is nothing. Momentarily I pity
him, and then dismiss the thought. He owes me something.

Together we make for the ridge of pale gold cliffs lining
the eastern horizon of Akhetaten. We walk on a dry river-
bed, and pass the silent tombs of the royal family and the
nobles of Akhetaten — empty shells waiting to be infused
with life by the death of those whose names are carved on
their walls.

We work our way through the mountains and pass out
into the wilderness beyond.

Heat and thirst make me exhausted and dizzy, but Ma-
nan leads on and I follow. The landscape is yellow,
vibrating with the heat; the sky blank and pitiless blue. The
Aten disk has no helpful hands to give us cups of water,
only rays like swords that cut into our flesh. We wear the
long desert cloaks of cotton and our heads are swathed, but
still I feel the heat will kill us if one of the desert cobras does

169

not. Ma-nan has insisted that I leave everything behind that could distinguish me as king, and when we occasionally meet a camp of desert nomads we are given hospitality like ordinary travellers, and like ordinary travellers searched thoroughly when we are alseep. Nothing is found but dusty cotton wraps, leather sandals and waterskins; and in the morning we are sent on our way with supplies of meat and drink.

Soon even the nomads cease to appear and we are alone, held to the hot, flat land by the huge suffocating hand of the sky. I have long since ceased to trust Ma-nan or not to trust him. We hardly speak, but make our way as best we can, thinking only of how we can get through the day without collapsing. Only at night my thoughts expand beyond this, and we lie side by side on the sand looking up at the stars. I think of all I have learned, and know that I have not begun to ask all the questions I want to ask — nor ever will. I may know the name of everything in our world and beyond: I may learn to weigh the stars and understand the nature of disease, so that no one will die of it; but I will still not know *why . . . why. . . .*

I wonder if Ma-nan thinks these thoughts, or whether he lies plotting my death. I no longer care. The questions of who shall rule and not rule, who shall worship and not worship, who shall love and not love no longer torment me. Life is stripped down to survival or not survival: the outcome a matter of chance.

I sit up suddenly in a huge darkness and wonder about this thought. Is it so? Is the answer to all the questions no more than this? Ma-nan has wandered off, and I could be alone on the earth waiting for the dice to fall.

There was the void. Why did it become non-void? Why?

I strain my eyes to see into the darkness, hoping that something, someone, will answer me.

I feel totally alone. Lonely beyond belief.

I am conscious: but conscious of nothing.

I am thinking: but have no thoughts.

I am alive: but have no extension in time and space.

It is as though I am the god who was alone in the great dark and was lonely: who said: "Let there be OTHER", and there was OTHER: who then enjoyed this otherness, and was no longer lonely.

Ra utters a syllable of light, and the sand and the hills and the rocks gradually become visible. Lying below me in a little valley I see the bones of a man picked clean by the vultures. Behind them Ma-nan is squatting, himself like a vulture in his black cotton cloak. I run down to him through the cool sand, and know that I have found my brother, his legs buckled and broken beneath him, his arms flung out beside him, the skull grinning. He is as clean and dry as crystal.

Ma-nan watches me from the shadow of his hood.

I am suddenly at a loss to know what to do. When a pharaoh dies there is always a structure of accepted procedure and ritual to rely on, a hierarchy of officials each with his own duties to perform, an elaborate pattern of movement and sound, of spell and prayer, each tiny part of which is believed to be vital to the survival of the man in the after-life. Akhenaten has been denied all this — how can I alone hope to take its place?

I look at Ma-nan. "Help me," I say. He has been a priest most of his life, though he has long abused the privilege.

He shifts from one haunch to the other but says nothing.

I am suddenly angry. I need his knowledge. I have never presided at a funeral before. He has. I approach him and seize his shoulder roughly, pulling him upright. As I do so his cloak falls away from his face. I am looking into the eyes, not of Ma-nan, but of Khurahtaten. I start back, shocked.

"Where is Ma-nan?" I demand.

"Here."

"No!" I cry. It can't be.

"This is the second duel," he says. "It is my turn now to question *you*."

My mouth is hanging open and I am staring like an idiot.

He draws a circle in the sand, as I had done before, this time to contain the two of us and the bones of Akhenaten.

"Look at him," he says quietly. I turn my head and look into the eye sockets of my brother, friend and king. I see Khurahtaten there too.

I am questioned step by step about my life, my love for my brother, for my brother's wife, for my brother's daughter. I am questioned about my motives for being king; my motives for planning the reforms I intend to make.

Gradually as the sun climbs higher I feel myself becoming dry and empty. Every pretence I have put up, has been knocked down; every lie I have told myself, has been uncovered. I stand at last in the full blaze of the sun at noon, naked of everything I have believed about myself, knowing that I am no better than the least among my subjects, knowing that I have failed miserably, through fear, through desire, through laziness and procrastination, to achieve the task I had accepted.

I can think of nothing but of lying down beside my brother and being wiped off the face of the earth with him. I have had an opportunity not given lightly, and have wasted it.

Khurahtaten looms over me like a giant, his head blocking out the sun so that I cannot see his features . . . but around him the rays blaze out.

"*Now*," he says, and the voice that had been so cold and relentless before, softens. "Now, my friend, you are ready to help your brother."

Help him? How can I help him, when I myself deserve oblivion?

Khurahtaten steps out of the circle and vanishes. I am alone in a vast wilderness with the broken bones of my friend, my partner . . . I kneel beside him weeping.

When I cease at last, exhausted, and sit back on my haunches, I know what prayer I must say, and to whom, to free my brother from the imprisoning spell of the false priests — it is written on no papyrus, chiselled on no walls. I know also that life and death have their own logic and are unaffected by long and elaborate rituals. I wish my friend and I could talk together as we did all those years ago beside the lake at Per-hay — now older, wiser, knowing what we know about ourselves.

It seems to me I feel his presence beside me. It seems to me I hear his voice in my own thoughts. There is no sense of defeat. No sense of loss. I am confident that the body of Akhenaten may have been broken by enemies and picked clean by vultures — but his spirit lives on.

Weariness and sleep overcome me at last, and when I wake Ma-nan is beside me, digging a grave for Akhenaten. As we bury him in the sand I pray as he taught me to pray: "I have come with praise to the Aten, the living and sole God, Lord of rays for giving light. I have come with love in my heart for thy child, issued from thy rays, Son of the Sun, living in truth, Akhenaten. Thou hast given eternity to him, thou art indeed the living Ra, who produced Maat, truth, justice. May he travel freely to the gates of the otherworld. May he see Ra at dawn when he rises in the eastern horizon, and may he see Aten when he sets on the western horizon of heaven. . . . May he take changing forms as a living soul. May he go out and in at the bidding of his heart."

Ma-nan watches and does nothing to avert the power of the words as they flow over the bones of the dead Pharaoh. . . .

Is it my imagination or does the sunlight suddenly flare up around us? I look up, startled, and see the outline of a huge bird winging its way towards the sun.

We turn for home, as silent as we were on the journey out,

but now for different reasons. I ponder that Khurahtaten had taken the form of Ma-nan and then of Akhenaten himself. And then I put the thought aside. In the night the howling of a dog to the full moon may make a man question his soul; in the day, the silver spray from the landing of a duck on water. Who knows what form the Questioner may take? Who knows when he will come?

The Destruction

My mind is full of plans for the future; how I will stand up
to Horemheb, how I will follow through the task my
brother and I had been set; how I, Sothis: I, Smenkhkare-
djeserkhepru, beloved of Akhenaten, will make sure the
religion of my people is a true religion, and not a beautiful
mask over an ugly and cruel face. I feel strong, confident,
capable of great deeds. I know I will not see Khurahtaten
again. He has done for me what he can, and now I must
stand alone.

My heart is singing and my feet tread lightly on the
burning sand. How beautiful the sky, how light and high
and full of joy! What scope we humans have, I think, what
infinite potential!

But just before we enter the cleft in the mountains,
through which we must pass before we can see the plains
of Akhetaten, I experience a strong sense of foreboding.

I look at Ma-nan, wondering if he has suddenly reverted
to his old ways and is working his spells on me, but he is
plodding behind me, wearily, not thinking of anything but
how he can take the next step. I tell him that I intend to
hurry on ahead, and that he should take his time. He nods
with some relief. I begin to stride and soon leave him far
behind.

As the heat of the day builds up my pace slackens, and I am forced to rest for a few moments. I doze in the shadow of a thorn bush and fall into a kind of half-sleep, waking from it with a jerk, convinced that I have seen Merytaten lying in a pool of blood. I force myself to travel on in spite of the heat.

At last the plain of Akhetaten lies before me in a haze of white light. From the limestone ridge that holds the tombs of the nobles I can see the gleam of the distant river, the city shimmering in the heat, unreal, insubstantial, mirage-like — as though one blink, and the whole rich and marvellous creation could disappear for ever.

I know there is something wrong. I can feel it. I look across the farmers' fields, squared off neatly by the canals, to the city streets, the low houses, and beyond them to the palace complex and the temple. I sense it is here that the troubles. There are no pennants fluttering: the breath of Aten is stilled.

I hurry down, the rough, loose stones hurting my feet, grazing my shins, yellow dust following me like a plume of smoke. People seem to be rushing from the city, carrying all their worldly possessions — donkeys overloaded, wives with bundles on their heads larger than themselves, and strings of children tugging at their skirts. . . . A scene that normally in the heat of the day would be somnolent and peaceful is now all movement and agitation. As I reach them I call out, but they take no notice of me. I can almost smell their fear. Deeper in the town, I find a shopkeeper wringing his hands beside his ruined shop, all his wares strewn across the street as though looters have been at work, and in their haste have dropped most of their booty. Earthenware jars are smashed, wine soaking like blood into the dust. His face is streaked with tears, his shoulders and his body bruised and cut.

"What has happened?" I cry.

He shakes his head, but I cannot catch what he mutters. I

176

pause for a moment, trying to make sense of what he is saying, but my fears are growing, and I run from him towards the temple before I have understood a word. I pass people grouped anxiously at street corners, shouting and arguing. In the street outside the temple a huge crowd has gathered, staring and pointing. The great doors are broken open, the masts that held the pennants so bravely high are smashed and splintered. I push past them. In my dusty cotton robes I am indistinguishable from them. I am invisible. No one would think that I am pharaoh of the Two Lands, First Prophet of the Great God Aten.

In the sacred court I find the bodies of my priests and servants, slain, the altar to the god overturned. Horrified, I run through the sacred precincts seeking some comfort in all the desolation. There is none. The key words of the beautiful prayers have been defaced and hammered out. Whoever did this knew what they were doing. This is no random vandalism. The temple has been carefully and systematically rendered powerless, the symbolic meaning of every part of it desecrated: the lifeline of its energy-flow cut.

I turn, in deep despair, and pass through the open doors again, pushing through the crowds.

Like a sleepwalker I make for my home.

The garden has been ravaged. Plants and bushes have been torn up and scattered: the irrigation channels have been breached, and the flood has destroyed the fragile pavilion where Merytaten and I have so often rested in the shade.

I take the steps to the palace three at a time, dreading what I will find.

I find Merytaten as I saw her in premonition — in the throne-room, her throat slit, her face still contorted with fear. Beside her, as though they had reached for protection and comfort from each other at the last moment, lies the body of Nefertiti.

177

Stunned, I stand and stare. Everywhere there are bodies of servants, of high officials — all those who had remained loyal to my brother and myself, and had not had the foresight to flee when the first signs of the changing times had appeared.

There is no sign anywhere of those who have wrought this havoc. Angrily I weep, and smash my fists against the walls.

Then, exhausted, I sit beside the two women I love, my arms around my knees, rocking like a frightened and lonely child. *What a waste, what a waste.* A waste of the past . . . a waste of the future.

Night falls and I sit on in the dark, mourning. I can no longer see the figures of the two women that lie beside me, so cold and pale. I see them as they were, beautiful as the sunlight on lotus, and as ephemeral. So you are all gone now, I think, all whom I have loved. My king, my brother, the women of my heart. Where are you now? Where will I find you? I have been crowned pharaoh, but I sit in the dirt in a cotton cloak with neither crown, nor cobra eye, nor crook nor flail. Even Nefertiti's crown has been ripped from her head, and it is only congealed blood that rings her forehead now. Without regalia, a man is hard put to it to prove that he is a king, or a woman to prove that she is a queen.

Tutankhaten? I have no hate for the boy, though I suspect all this has been done for him. He is to be used in a game played by ruthless men. If he makes one false move, his fate will be the same as ours. I wonder who will be regent until he comes of age to rule? Horemheb? If so, the boy will never reach maturity, for Horemheb will never be content to step down.

I sit among the dead in the ruined hall all night, thinking . . . thinking. . . . I do not wish to be pharaoh — but I am loath to abandon the Two Lands to the rule of someone who could do what has been done this day in Akhetaten.

In the morning when those who are left in the city are still behind closed shutters, I carry the bodies of Merytaten and Nefertiti to the river. The river flows as it has always flowed, deep and true, uncorrupted by the motives and the deeds of men. It flows from the unknown to the unknown, bringing life. The prayers I say over the two women as I lower them into the arms of the river clothe them more surely in the love of God than any golden mask or funeral bandages.

I sit a long time on the bank watching the flow of the water. I am weary of life: yet I must not give it up.

Later that day I set off for Waset as an ordinary man, a refugee from the stricken city, taken on board his boat by a merchant with other refugees. He does not know that I am pharaoh, and I do not tell him. He tells me that the true god, Amun, is to be fully restored in his rightful place at the head of the hierarchy, and all local deities are to be honoured as before. The merchant seems unconcerned about the upheaval his country is going through, and worries only about how it will affect his livelihood. He seems to think trade will be brisker under the new regime, and that there are fortunes to be made in the marketing of statuettes and amulets.

"Plenty of new building, too," he says. "Work for everyone."

"What of the people murdered at Akhetaten?" I ask. "Was that not a terrible thing?"

"A terrible thing," he agrees. "But Amun was rightfully angry."

"They say the new Pharaoh did not deny Amun completely," I protest.

He looks suspiciously at me, and wants to know if I am a supporter of Akhenaten. I know what will happen to me if I admit to it.

179

"No," I lie.

The merchant, of course, has not seen the sights I have seen. He will not carry in his heart for ever the sight of those so cruelly slain. He rides on the crest of rumour and Horemheb's propaganda without question.

He tells me later that Tutankhaten is to be crowned as pharaoh before the full moon and Ay is to be his regent until he is old enough to reign properly. I am glad to hear that Ay is to be regent, and not Horemheb.

"Prince Tutankhaten should have been pharaoh right away after the heretic's death," the merchant gossips on. "But that upstart Smenkhkare, the heretic's lover-boy, pushed himself forward and grabbed the throne. Who believes that rubbish about him having royal blood in his veins? No one heard anything about that in the old king's lifetime."

"But even if he was not the old king's son by a royal wife, he was married to Queen Nefertiti and to the heiress Merytaten."

The merchant spits and an expletive indicates what he thinks of that.

I look at the changeless hills as the boat slides past them on the blue water, and ponder the changeability of the affairs of man in contrast.

How many times have I travelled this route to Waset, and each time has been more extraordinary than the last. What awaits me now in this city of Amun? I am afraid. The merchant's words ring in my ears. All that had seemed sacred and beautiful and good to us who lived in the light of the Aten is now said to be blasphemous, ugly and evil. How quickly the switch is made and how powerless we are against the prejudices of others. I feel like the one sane man in a group of lunatics, their word taken against his only because there are more of them.

In the city of Waset there is an atmosphere of tremendous

180

excitement. Horemheb's troops strut about the streets, cheered by crowds feverishly showing their support for the new regime. The pennants are up on the gateways to the temple of Amun-Ra.

I leave the merchant, and mingle with the crowd, trying not to be recognized. I need not have worried: Smenkhkare is assumed dead, with the rest of the heretic criminals in the City of Sin. Everyone seems pleased that at last a real pharaoh, a true son of the mighty Amenhotep Nebma'atre' and his Great Royal Wife Tiye, is to reign. The golden age is about to begin! I am told that the nameless heretic and his equally nameless disgusting male lover consorted with dogs and goats and monkeys, as well as each other. The only comfort in all this is that the good names of Nefertiti and her daughters seem not to have been treated in the same way. They are described as having been misled and misused by the two male perverts. Nefertiti and her daughter Merytaten are supposed to have taken their own lives in Akhetaten. The younger daughters and Ankhesen-paaten are in Waset, the latter to become the Great Royal Wife of Tutankhaten. It is rumoured that Akhenaten was not only depraved, but deformed and sterile as well, and that Nefertiti's daughters were not his.

I wander about the city like a ghost.

I see the young prince being carried in a golden litter. His face is so covered with paint, and his body enveloped in such rich garments, I can hardly believe it is the same young lad I saw not so long ago, swimming joyfully naked like a brown fish, in the lake at Meru-Aten. He was laughing then. Now his face is pinched and tired, his eyes have the glazed look mine used to have when Ma-nan had been busy with his special smoke.

I glimpse a dark figure hurrying through the streets, and I am convinced that it is Ma-nan. I follow him. He slips down crowded alleys and I almost lose him. At last he taps on the huge wooden door of a mansion. When the door is opened I am just behind him, and I slip in with him, touching him on the shoulder. I suppose desperation has made me reckless. It is certainly a foolish thing to do.

Even now he does not turn and show his face, but hurries across the courtyard. At the other side he stops as a tall figure emerges from the house. Now he turns. It *is* Ma-nan, but beside him is Na-aghta. I can see that he has reverted to how he used to be. How shallow his conversion must have been! No, not so shallow. I see in his eyes that he now has shame for what he does, where before he had pride. Na-aghta has him by the arm, and I can see that he holds him tightly, as though he too is not sure whether he has complete control or not. Ma-nan looks at me, silently pleading for forgiveness. The mood of the country has changed, and he has now the chance to be a power in the land again. He yearns for power as much as he always did — but I know, and he knows, he will never have the pleasure in it again that he once had. I feel a kind of pity for him, and detachment from my own fear.

I walk calmly towards them. Perhaps I believe even now I can make changes if I but say the right words.

I hear the huge bolts of the door drawn behind me, see Na-aghta signal with his eyes to someone behind and to the right of me. Ma-nan suddenly moves and pulls away from him, running towards me, shouting a warning.

But it is too late.

I hardly feel the spear go in my back, and stand for a moment staring with amazement at the point of it protruding from my chest.

Will it be so bad to die? I had wanted to die so passionately once. Perhaps I do again.

Ah, but to die with a task unfinished!

It is only when I notice the triumphant face of Na-aghta

and Ma-nan kneeling over me, weeping, that I know that
I am dead.

* * *

Let your wings be my wings
O Horus, the sun's companion.
Teach me the currents of the air . . .
the high spiral
of the sky's heart . . .
the breathless pause
as the earth holds still
for the god to speak.

Fear has held my feet to the ground.
Fear has weighed me down.
My eyes and ears are blind and deaf with dust.

Immortal Bird
shake me free,
turn me loose
in your splendour. . . .
Under your protection
let me soar.
Let me see the sun before its rising.
Let me see the world
at the point of transformation.

Notes

Marriage alliances important in this book

Amenhotep III (Nebma'atre'): to Queen Tiye and to his eldest daughter Sitamon.

Amenhotep IV (Akhenaten): to Nefertiti and to his daughter Ankhesenpaaten.

185

Smenkhkare: to Merytaten and to Nefertiti.

Tutankhamun: to Ankhesenpaaten.

Ay (Queen Tiye's brother): to Nefertiti's mother, to Tey (Nefertiti's nurse/step-mother), and finally on becoming pharaoh, to Ankhesenpaaten.

Horemheb: to Nezem-mut (Mudnodjme) — Nefertiti's sister.

Modern equivalents of place-names used in this story

Ancient Egyptian: Modern
Kemet; The Two Lands: Egypt
Men-Nefer: Memphis
Lunu; On: Heliopolis (a suburb of Cairo)
Waset: Thebes
Ipet-Esut: Karnak
Ipet-Resut: Luxor
Akhetaten: Tel el Amarna
Khmun: Hermopolis (now el-Ashmunein)
Per-hay: Malkata
Djahi: Syria; Palestine

A king list of the Eighteenth Dynasty
(adapted from *Atlas of Ancient Egypt* by John Baines and Jaromír Málek, Phaidon Press, 1958)

Ahmose	1550–1525 BC
Amenhotep I	1525–1504 BC
Thutmose I	1504–1492 BC
Thutmose II	1492–1479 BC
Thutmose III	1479–1425 BC
Hatshepsut	1473–1458 BC
Amenhotep II	1427–1401 BC
Thutmose IV	1401–1391 BC
Amenhotep III (Nebma'atre')	1391–1353 BC
Amenhotep IV / Akhenaten	1353–1335 BC
Smenkhkare	1335–1333 BC
Tutankhamun	1333–1323 BC
Ay	1323–1319 BC
Horemheb	1319–1307 BC